# Exit Stage Left

## PATTI LARSEN

Exit Stage Left
Patti Larsen

Copyright 2013 by Patti Larsen

Purely Paranormal Press

Find out more about Patti Larsen at
www.pattilarsen.com
Sign up for new releases
bit.ly/pattilarsenemail

ISBN-13: 978-1927464618
ISBN-10: 1927464617

Cover art (copyright) by Christina G Gaudet. All rights reserved.
www.christinaggaudet.com

Edited by Annetta Ribken, freelance Goddess. You can find her at
www.wordwebbing.com

# Also By Patti Larsen

*The Hayle Coven Novels*
*The Nightshade Cases*
*The Clone Chronicles*
*The Diamond City Trilogy*
*And much, much more*

Find your next favorite author at
www.pattilarsen.com
or her books at
www.purelyparanormalpress.com

## *Dedication*

To my dear friend and writer-in-crime, Kimberly Kinrade, for convincing me this was a good idea. She was right.

# Prologue

She sits at his death bed, holding his hand, limp and cold, already lifeless despite the slow, steady beeping of the monitor. Her thumb traces over the back, his skin so thin she used to be able to see his veins, blue tracery of spider-webbed life. Those are sunken, now, just his pale, pale flesh left behind. And his bones, jutting from what remains of him.

They said goodbye long before he slipped into his final coma. Before this trip to the hospital when the doctors told him, sad and quiet, it would be his last. Even before the cancer came back and he had to start more treatments.

They'd been saying goodbye for years. In the only ways they knew how. Soft kisses in the dark under the stars, on a blanket in the yard while his parents gave them space. Whispered conversations in the back seat of her car where they sat for hours, steaming the inside of the windows in the pouring rain. Texts and phone calls when they couldn't be together, hugs and smiles and sweet silence only they felt when they could.

And yet, this goodbye hurts her more than she expected.

Because it is their last.

She lays her head on his shoulder, feels the give of his weak body, the harshness of his breath. No life support. No heroic measures for the one she loves, a hero in her *eyes already. Stronger than she will ever be.*

*And when his chest rises for the last time, she stops breathing, too. Can't hear the sound of the single strobing alarm from the monitor, his mother's sharp cry as she falls over him on the other side of the bed, sobbing.*

*The outside world means nothing to her.*

*His soul is gone.*

*And she is certain hers will never heal.*

# Chapter One

I stuff a t-shirt into a tiny hole I find in the corner of my second bag and straighten up, lower back aching from hunching over for what seems like days. I think I've successfully crammed what consists of my life into two suitcases, a laptop bag, and a backpack I dug out from the back of my closet. High school leftovers, still with some old exams at the bottom, *A's* circled in red.

It feels like forever ago.

My thumb skirts the daisy drawn in blue ink, the edges a little wobbly, stem stunted and crooked. His favorite flower. Mine, too. Though this one has its issues.

Ian was always a terrible artist, though he tries.

Tried.

I cough, pretending it's dust giving me the sniffles, and shove the remains of my graduating year into the wastebasket beside my small desk. I take a look around my room.

Not much left. I'm not taking my comforter. Aunt Vonda already bought me a new one in her excitement to have me live with her, so that's covered. Dad can put my books and old knickknacks from when I was a kid in storage. When he gets around to it.

If he gets around to it.

Who am I kidding? I hike the backpack over my shoulder, already aching with the effort of lifting the massive bag, and clench my teeth together. *If Dad even notices I'm gone, it will be a miracle.*

The first suitcase thuds down the stairs behind me as I pant to a halt and release the handle. It totters, overfull, and falls on its side, rocking on the rounded front like an upside down turtle. I'm out of shape, my body protesting as I dump the backpack and walk back upstairs for the rest.

I stop in my room one more time. Catch my breath, lost not to exertion but to a wash of memory.

I can clearly see Ian lying on my bed, thin body weak, but a smile on his face.

*Come here and kiss me*, his phantom says, one hand hiding the shunt under his shirt so I won't have to have the reminder. Because he is awesome like that.

Until a year ago. When "is" became "was".

I have to get the hell out of here.

My phone chimes with a text from Courtney.

*Hve FUN! :D Miss U.*

I don't bother answering my one-time BFF, lugging the next bag out of my room, the corner catching on the doorframe.

"Shit." I jerk on it too hard, the bag pulling free so fast it loses balance, twists sideways. Takes my wrist with it. I release it and let it fall while I hike up my breath and refuse to cry over my hurt.

Either of my hurts. Because it's not just my wrist that's aching.

Dad's downstairs. I hear him in the kitchen, right below me. Just like him not to help, not to even offer or acknowledge I'm leaving. I wipe at my nose with the shoulder of my t-shirt, finally able to breathe. *Exhale. Inhale.* Let my shoulders drop.

Let Ian's memory rest yet again. At least for a little while.

Until something reminds me the love of my life is gone and I'll never, ever see him again. Hold him. Whisper his name in his ear while his hazel eyes tell me he loves me.

*Rye,* his lips say in my memory.

It's become so ordinary to torture myself. I lose time in the quiet of the hall. Dad drops something below, the sound of shattering glass shaking me free of Ian. I square my shoulders and swipe at my tears as my father curses and bangs a cupboard door shut, reminding me about the other reason I'm leaving.

My phone vibrates again. Courtney.

*See U in the city?* ☺

Yeah, right. And though Courtney might not really give a shit about what I'm doing, only wanting a place to crash when she and her posse come to the city on weekends, she is right. This is supposed to be fun. A new start for me. Away from home and the grief I feel living in Clifton, surrounded by Ian. Weighted down by my father's disapproval and disdain for the last year.

Off to New York and adventure.

Twenty-one. Broken hearted.

Moving on.

I scowl at the suitcase and kick it firmly with the toe of my shoe.

Whatever. Still, the small act of violence makes me feel better. I wrestle the big bag upright on its knobby wheels and roll it to the stairs. Man-handle it to the bottom, shoulder brushing the edge of a photograph. I gasp as the frame slips, releasing my hold on the suitcase. My fingers catch the edge of the picture, just saving it from falling, but at the sacrifice of the suitcase, which bangs and smashes its way to the hardwood floor below.

But the photo is safe in my hands, now clutched to my chest. The sound of feet thud toward me. I look up from my mother's smiling face to see Dad come to a halt, looming over my things.

Scowling. As usual.

"Riley, what are you doing?" His harsh voice is no surprise. He hasn't said a kind word to me for years. Like I give a crap.

I hang the picture back in its place, carefully leveling it by eye, hating to frown at Mom while I answer Dad, but unable to keep anger from my face. Funny how no matter what I do it pisses him off.

I purposely push his buttons, wanting to strike at him for being a jackass and not lifting a finger to help me. "Nothing." I feel the tension growing between us with that one word. He hates one word answers. It's very satisfying to kiss Mom goodbye with my lips to my fingertips and then to her face before I turn and stomp my way to the ground floor. Refusing to meet his eyes as I shoulder my backpack, anger cresting, feeling suddenly frustrated and furious without knowing the main reason why.

I don't need just one reason. I have a million. The biggest one stands in front of me, arms crossed over his chest, face a dark cloud. His buzzed hair making him look old with nothing to soften the dark tan on his face, the frown lines around his eyes, the pull downward of his mouth. He towers over me, my fireman father, no hero in my eyes.

Just a damned bully. Watching instead of helping.

Asshole.

"I don't want to hear you've been partying and giving your aunt grief." I almost laugh in his face.

Suppressing the urge to strike out at him, knowing it's not worth it. We've been on this ride before so many times I barely muster enough energy to shrug.

Instead, I choose to jerk the giant bag I dropped upright and examine it. The last party I'd been to was with Ian.

*You know me so well, don't you?*

At least the suitcase hadn't split, there was a bonus. I had to sit on it to close it, so luck was on my side.

I walk away from my father, the rattle of the bag's wheels loud behind me, drowning out the ominous silence. Still no help from him as I leverage open the screen door with one foot, grunting to pull open the heavy steel one. Manage.

On my own.

I guess that's a good sign, too.

I teeter down the three concrete steps to the walkway with my life on a leash trailing behind me. The suspension in the back of my little hatchback groans under the weight of the bag when I finally dump it into the trunk. Panting and sweating in the early June heat, I wipe at my upper lip, the beads of moisture. Great start to a three hour drive.

Dad stands in the entry, almost blocking me. *Really? Are we going to continue playing this game, today of all days?* I push past him, flinching from the contact as his bare arm brushes mine, and into the house.

Find my second bag waiting at the door.

Finally, some help. And a clear sign telling me to get the hell out.

I'm happy to oblige.

"You're going to look at colleges while you're in New York." Not a question. Like he thinks he can tell me what to do. But it's the first time Dad's said anything about what I'm doing, where I'm going. He barely responded when I told him Aunt Vonda—his own sister for God's sake—invited me to come live with her, "For the change of scenery, pet," she said.

I hate the sudden intrusion, his show of interest. This flash of fatherly whatever he seems to think is appropriate after ignoring me my entire life. Since when does he get a say?

Dad half-turns, the light behind him as I wrench the second bag to my side, snatch my purse from the hall table. Shoulder my laptop. I can't help but glare.

"That's the plan," I say, not wanting to start a fight after all, though I know one is brewing. I feel it in both of us. But I don't have time to argue.

I just need to go already.

Dad must agree with me, because he doesn't snap back. Just nods. But he holds his ground, doesn't move. I'm about to bowl him over with my suitcase when he finally stands back, as if we've just been in some stupid standoff he's choosing to let me win.

He holds the door open for me.

"See you, then," he says.

I hate him so much in that moment, my stomach heaves, tightens into a giant knot. The only thing saving me is the wide open door and the freedom beyond it. From Dad, from my memories.

So why does it still hurt there is no hug goodbye from her daddy for Riley James?

It's not until I'm in the car, driving away, hands clenched on the steering wheel, I allow the sobs begging to escape to build in my chest and I finally let them out.

# Chapter Two

The tears blur my departure as I turn from my old street and down the block. Pass Ian's house. I said goodbye to his parents, Susan and Dwight, this morning already. But it doesn't stop me from looking as I drive by, just in case.

I shouldn't be so upset about my dad. I have parents, in Ian's. The most amazing people I've ever met, who love me still. They were the ones to encourage me on this crazy journey.

"You need to find yourself," Susan said the night she and Dwight sat me down to suggest it. "Ian wanted you to live, Rye."

It was a long time before I wanted to. But they were right. I really do have to go.

I wave despite knowing they aren't aware I'm doing it, blow them a kiss. Deliberately take Elm Street past the cemetery. Park and breathe before scooping up the handful of daisies I stole from the neighbor's yard and slam the car door behind me.

Ian's grave is close to the road. His family one of the oldest in town. It means I don't have to go far to reach him.

The stone is really beautiful, black marble. He

picked it out six months before he died.

"I can't leave everything to Mom and Dad," he said as he ran his hand over the sample in the showroom. It grossed me out headstone places had a showroom, like they were selling cars or furniture, not markers of death. I wanted to leave, but his smile held me, as usual. His casual acceptance. And the way Ian made me laugh as he draped himself over the headstone, making his so-called zombie face.

I crouch in front of the real thing, wishing I was back there with him now. That I could rewind time and hug him again. Kiss him. Find a way to stop the leukemia from coming back. No superpowers appear, just like no miracle did for him, despite the drug trials and herb treatments and endless chemo and radiation.

An old, dead bundle of daisies lies to the side, my last offering, nestled lovingly beside the giant pile of flowers Susan tends so carefully. So sweet of her not to discard my meager attempt at keeping Ian company. I do the job for her, tossing the brown mess aside, settling the new bundle where the old had been.

I pinch off a daisy head and tuck it behind my ear, just like Ian always did.

"I guess..." I fight for words, trying to think of something clever, because Ian would love that, but failing. "I'll see you." Dad's words.

The wind picks up. It blows over me in a soft breeze, ruffles my hair, kisses my cheek. Gone as quickly as it came.

One more tear escapes, trickles. I snuffle, wipe it away.

Press my lips to his headstone. "Love you," I whisper.

My car waits for me, low in the back, the inside baking with heat when I slip inside. My iffy air conditioning gives me a break and pumps out a blast of cold before settling on luke-warm. The frames of my sunglasses are hot against my skin, but they hide the red rims of my eyes and make it easier to believe, when I don them, I really am going on an adventure.

And not leaving my heart behind.

Classic tunes fill the interior as I blast the stereo, the only reliable part of the whole car, pumping Queen and Meatloaf and Mom's favorite ABBA over and through me, the pounding bass vibrating my seat as I sing at the top of my lungs to clear my head.

Works wonders. I barely flinch as I drive past the park where Ian and I used to hang out when he couldn't go far. And the coffee shop where we drank endless cups and talked and laughed when it rained.

Every "where Ian and I" flies by until the highway beckons.

As I pass the "Thank you for visiting beautiful Clifton, New York," I choke. I can't help it. Bark out one last sob, tearing at my chest, making my eyes burn, my lungs heave as my diaphragm protests.

And then it's over and I'm merging into traffic.

*This is going to be awesome, you know.* His memory sits in the seat beside me, an apparition no stranger to my times alone. I glance at him, nod. Knowing it's crazy to cling to him like this, but missing my best friend so much I just can't bring myself to release him.

Not yet. And maybe not ever.

A sign tells me it's 186 miles to Manhattan. I push the gas pedal down and commit to my new life even as my make-believe Ian smiles in the passenger seat beside me.

I pull over and stock up on chocolate and chips at a gas station, buying all of Ian's favorites because they are mine, too. Munching and singing—hearing his voice clearly butchering every song just like he used to—I start to feel an odd sensation in the pit of my stomach. But it's not until I pass a giant line of tractor trailers and catch another sign I realize what I'm feeling.

117 miles to go.

It's excitement.

The realization startles me. Am I? Am I really excited to leave home, leave Ian, everything I know? But no, not everything. He's beside me, isn't he? My lips pull into a smile as Heart sings *Barracuda* on my stereo. Ian's favorite song, the sound of his phantom's voice bellowing the words at the top of his lungs, so loud I laugh.

I can do this, then. Knowing he's coming with me after all. I've packed his memory, the moments alone I can imagine. He's still here, just like one of my t-shirts. I feared leaving Clifton behind, because I'd spent most of my life doing everything I could to keep Ian with me.

No complaints. I put my entire life on hold to make sure we had every moment together possible. My best guy friend since kindergarten when he was first diagnosed, my boyfriend since tenth grade, still suffering around short bouts of remission. Three years out of high school spent first taking care of him the best way I knew how—by being at his side as long and as often as I could—and shelving my own dreams.

Suddenly, I understand my guilt at abandoning him doesn't have to mean he's gone. The possibilities are endless. *Maybe I will check out schools. Make new friends. Make a new life.*

Something I've never really allowed myself, I now realize. My life was Ian. I don't regret a moment. I'm grateful every day for him. But this feels right. Moving on, my amazing love at my side whenever I need him.

Susan knew it. Dwight. I wonder if they'd worry knowing how I linger over their dead son's memory.

I push back my sunglasses, ponytail hitting the headrest as I smile into the blue sky and the road ahead, not really caring. I'm moving on. And I'm taking Ian with me.

*Love you, babe*, he says.

"I love you, too." My whisper disappears in the volume of the song.

I'm so lost in the music I almost miss my exit, tires squealing softly as I cut across two lanes and nearly side-swipe a van full of kids. I wince my apology, wave to the cursing driver and scoot forward, down the off ramp, still driving too fast. Adrenaline pumping, heart skipping, Ian laughing in my head—he loved it when I played the daredevil—I merge yet again into more traffic, the skyline now dominated by a bridge and high rises in the distance.

It's almost six o'clock by the time I follow the bumper-to-bumper line of cars across the Hudson River and onto Manhattan Island, leaving the mainland behind me.

I follow the parkway around the island. The river glitters on my right, the city growing from residential buildings to taller apartments and on toward the center of New York, towering over the rest on my left. I can imagine Ian rubber necking to get a good look. He loved coming to the city, though he rarely had the chance.

I'm going to explore it for him. With him. Make it our home.

I take a left on West 54th, spotting a little marquis on the side of a large brick building faced by lovely trees. The sight stirs a thrill in my stomach and I'm grinning all over again.

*Going to be a star, Riley James*, Ian's voice whispers.

While looking into colleges is one possibility while I'm here, I've been suppressing my real hope.

That I'll be able to start acting again.

Aunt Vonda did mention she lived on the outskirts of the theater district. I think I forced myself to forget. Just in case I didn't get the chance to step on a stage again.

*Dreams are made for living, babe*, Ian says.

I shrug off the memory. Time will tell. For now, I can smile at the chintzy blinking lights someone set up, the hand-painted sign proclaiming the show is "The best in town, says the *Chelsea-Clinton News*." And dream.

I glance at the post-it note I plastered to the dusty dash of my car, squinting at my own handwriting while dodging a yellow cab that jerks to an abrupt halt in front of me. I make a right turn and drive for several blocks, liking the neighborhood already, the steps up to the doorways, the old trees shading the street. Finally, I pull up to a towering, old apartment building.

My phone is already ringing when I slip it out of my pocket. Aunt Vonda's face smiles back from her avatar when I hit answer.

"Hey, Auntie," I say with a smile in my voice. "I'm out front. I think."

She laughs, a little high pitched, ending in a soft snort. "I'm looking at that miserable excuse you have for a car," she says. "I'll be right down."

I hang up, still grinning. Exit the driver's seat to a blast of cooler air, realizing only then the inferno I've been sitting in. Not that it matters when Aunt Vonda comes bouncing out the big wooden front entry and down the steps, her generous boobs bobbing as she rushes to the sidewalk. She leaps over the curb into traffic, gives the guy who honks the finger before dashing to my side and crushing me in her arms.

I hug her back, shaking for some reason, feeling every emotion possible as my old hurt wells up in my throat and tries to expel itself all over her. It's tough to hold back despite the hope of my drive. Seeing her makes me think of Dad. Mom. And the fact Ian really is gone, my fantasy bubble shattered yet again.

I manage to hold it together. By the time Aunt Vonda lets me go, beaming as she grips my face between her hands, I'm smiling again, if barely.

"Darling pet," she says. Kisses my cheek with her pink lipstick. Dad got all the height in their family, my aunt at least six inches shorter than me. But she kept all the heart. I think it's a better trade all around.

"You look more like your mother every time I see you." Aunt Vonda hugs me again before sighing happily while I struggle with more tears. It's fine, I'm used to pretending everything is okay, only losing it after the illusions fade and I'm confronted with reality. There have been times in the last year I've broken down, unable to stop for what felt like days. But I'm really hoping this move will mean the end to those events.

Considering I've spent the last three hours pretending Ian is alive and with me, I know it's not a very good beginning.

Aunt Vonda squeezes herself into the passenger seat of my car and I almost snap. She fills Ian's place, grunting as she shoves the remains of my junk binge aside. I didn't notice the black box in her hand, only spotting it when she waves at the alley beside the building.

I follow her directions, pulling across the street and into the back lot as she chatters at me while I do my best to control the unreasonable anger I feel.

As though she's broken the last of my connection to Ian.

"I hope you like your room, I made it up special. I know how much you love daisies, so I bought a quilt with daisies on it." Her bubbly chatter prods me out of my temper and into amusement. I almost laugh as she rushes on. "Okay, go down here." She points at the ramp, guiding me to a pair of steel doors. "You can park in my second spot as long as you want." I'm not planning on using my car much, hoping to get around on foot or use public transit as much as possible. My hatchback is known to quit now and then, and after the long drive we'd just had, I don't want to risk it.

Besides, it's a perfect chance for Ian and me to—

For me. For me to get to know the city.

I pull down into the darkness of the underground, following Vonda's pointing, finally slipping my little car in next to her minivan. *Fleur de Vonda* glares back with a huge, smiling image of her face, her website and phone number in flowery letters beneath.

"The pimpmobile," she rolls her eyes and laughs. "Johnny talked me into it." Her oldest son's job as an IT guy for the government must be stifling his creativity, because he is always at Aunt Vonda for something. New website, social media. She is more hooked up than I am.

"It's hot," I say with a wink, forcing myself to be normal and not a freak who fights an endless battle in her head with remembering her dead boyfriend is dead. The van really is atrocious. I just pray she doesn't want me to drive it.

Aunt Vonda is already out, the passenger door squealing as she shoves it open, the hinge protesting such abrupt behavior. I pat the dash and whisper thanks for the car's faithful service before climbing out, stretching. The air of the garage is cool, tainted by the smell of oil and mustiness, but a welcome change from the heat of the car.

With Aunt Vonda's help, it only takes one trip up the cranky old elevator to the sixth floor and her apartment. We giggle together as we stuff ourselves in the tiny box, crammed with the two giant suitcases, and wave off a young couple who smile and let us go.

The hall on Aunt Vonda's floor is quiet and clean, much nicer than I expected from the outside of the building. And her door is painted a lovely deep green to match the rest in the hall. Shining gold numbers sparkle in the light as she breathlessly keys the lock.

Smiles at me over her shoulder.

"Welcome home, pet," she says. "I'm so happy to have you here." And opens the door.

# Chapter Three

I slip the dozen roses into a paper liner and staple it shut as the man in front of the counter nervously fiddles with his phone, barely looking up when I set them between us. My fingers straighten the little packet of preserver dangling from the top as I wait for him to notice me.

He doesn't even comment when I tell him he's laying out over a hundred bucks for flowers that will die in a week, his credit card out before I can repeat the price showing on the computer's readout. My perky smile doesn't register with him at all as he hustles out, scrawled signature crooked and off center on the slip of paper I slide into the drawer.

Aunt Vonda laughs over my shoulder into the quiet of the empty store as he leaves, bell jingling behind him. "He's in trouble," she says.

I turn from the aromatic and greenery-laden front to frown at her, though I'm half-smiling, too. "You're a flower whisperer, are you?"

Aunt Vonda winks at me from the back over the giant mound of wedding blossoms she's assembling, deft hands tucking ferns and leaves in a space I didn't even know required it until I see how awesome it looks placed there.

"You work in this business long enough," she says, "you get to understand people and their motivations."

"All through flowers." I turn as the doorbell rings again, brushing bits of rose ends from my pink apron and smile at the couple who wander through, looking at arrangements.

Aunt Vonda comes to my side, leans in, hands full of fern fronds. "Those two are buying for a funeral, my guess." I can see it then, the tightness around the woman's eyes and mouth, the way the man hovers over her. "Long illness," Aunt Vonda whispers. "Expected." She flinches a little, meets my eyes with her own sadness. Only then do I think of Ian.

And squeeze her arm. "Cool superpower," I say, smiling so she knows her remark doesn't bother me.

It really doesn't. Because he's with me all the time.

She sets aside her burden of ferns and goes to the couple, speaks softly to them while Ian's phantom leans over the counter, smiling sadly.

*Mom looked like that*, his ghost says. *When I died.*

She did, too. I remember Susan's tight, pinched expression, as though the tension in her face was the only thing holding back the torrent of tears. I knew from experience they wouldn't stop once they started or until she ran out of the will to cry.

I watch in shock as the strange woman's face crumples and she nods, allows Aunt Vonda to take her hand, the crushed whiteness of a wadded tissue appearing as she does.

And I realize my aunt is amazing.

I've already learned so much from her and it's only been a week. Hard for me to believe, really, seven days have gone by. I feel like I've been here forever, in a good way. Walking the streets of New York, exploring Broadway and Time's Square with Aunt Vonda on Sunday afternoon while Ian's memory trailed along, prodding me to ask questions and pay attention. To live. Layering memories over a life I knew I lived once.

In Clifton.

With him. And now here. No different, except I can't really hug him. And he's just a figment of my imagination.

Moving on, the change of scenery everyone said would do the job?

Did the job. At least as far as I'll allow.

Right from my first night, Aunt Vonda made me feel like her own daughter, though my cousin Caroline, her husband, and newborn son lived in Dubai.

"Really," Aunt Vonda moaned. "Stupid oil jobs. Why couldn't they have gone to Texas?" I grinned as she rolled her eyes, leading me through her spacious living room and open concept kitchen, down the hall to the back of the apartment. "At least then they'd still be in the U.S." She hesitated by my door, smiling at me, blinking away moisture in her eyes. "I hope you like it here, pet," she said, one hand settling on her cleavage. "I've missed having a girl around."

The room was small, but she wasn't kidding about the daisies. Comforter, pillow shams, even a cute decorative pillow in the shape of a daisy. I looked around the freshly painted blue walls and large window overlooking the street and smiled. Aunt Vonda squealed softly at my expression.

She steered me toward a narrow white door and into the small, but complete, bathroom on the other side.

"Not the princess suite," she said, voice

quivering, "but it should be okay?"

I spun and hugged her on the spot.

"It's perfect," I said. "Thank you so much."

And, a week later, it still is. I love my room and the breeze blowing in the window. My privacy for talking to Ian, who my mind sees laying on my bed more often than not, his quirky smile pulling at his mouth, closing over one eye almost all the way. Just like home.

The fact I can climb to the roof and the deck shared by the whole building, look out over Hell's Kitchen and the towering core of Manhattan not so far away is just an added bonus. Not to mention the easy three block walk to the flower shop and my job.

Perfect. Everything. Even more so when, three nights ago, Aunt Vonda dropped a magazine on the table beside me while I finished dinner. Sat with a hopeful smile pulling at her round cheeks, the lines narrowing her sparkling eyes. She nervously patted her curly red hair as I read the cover, Ian's phantom leaning over my shoulder to whisper the title in my ear.

"*Backstage*?"

*A trade magazine for theater and film in New York*, Ian said while my stomach flipped over.

"You mentioned acting classes," Aunt Vonda said, hands fluttering, her multitude of gold rings catching the light. "I thought you might want to have a look."

Since that moment, the magazine has been my best friend, as much as Ian's memory. I carry it with me everywhere, hear his voice talk about the hope living between its pages. There are times he distracts me with his excitement over it so much I'm lost for hours.

In fact, the magazine sits behind me right now as I wait for Aunt Vonda to handle the mourning couple. I reach out absently to touch Ian's hand. Feel cold glass and remember he's not really there.

I hate those moments most of all, the ones when I forget it's not real and Ian is just an apparition. Something I've constructed in my head to keep me from falling apart. To block the sudden sting of tears and reality, I spin and grab the magazine. I finger through it, absorbing myself in the write-ups, the images of actors and scenes frozen in time highlighting reviews of new shows. I love the listings, the articles. Everything about it feels magical, a portal to another world. To my dreams, the place where Ian lives. Silly how a classified ad for a sound technician could make my heart sing. Or a sprawling spread for a theater production could almost make me swoon.

This is my passion. And the last thing Ian spoke to me about. Just before he sank into the coma he never woke from.

"Rye," he said. "Go live your dream, now. I'll be cheering you on from wherever I am."

A tear hits the open page, spreads on the semi-gloss surface. Damn it, do I have to remember his death when I just want to cling to him as I have this past week? Doesn't matter the memory, really. Ian's wish—alive or imagined—is my command.

Now I just have to muster the courage to act instead of living inside the fantasy.

The doorbell rings. Aunt Vonda is still busy with the grieving woman and I shake off my imaginary moment under the lights, Ian clapping in the seats, to do my job.

I look up as four people stroll in. And catch my breath.

He is tall, lean, t-shirt faded, though it looks like it's on purpose. Dark blonde hair hangs in waves around his cheekbones, shoved back by one long-fingered hand. His jeans hang low on his narrow hips, but it's his eyes. Blue, so blue, like a summer sky just after it rains. And his smiling mouth.

He's smiling at me.

Aunt Vonda bumps into me, breaking my moment of awkward staring. I feel myself flush, hating it, knowing I'll be all blotchy down to my collarbone and suddenly wishing I could just let her handle it, handle him.

What the hell is wrong with me? He's just a guy. I've seen cute guys before. And he's not Ian. That truth slaps me with so much guilt I have to lean against the counter to stay upright even as my mind hunts for Ian's phantom.

Who remains absent, for once.

When I look up again, knowing I have to at least try to act normal, I realize handsome isn't alone. A stunning black girl, her full hair held back in a gold scarf, smiles at me, teeth a striking contrast with her dusky skin. She leans over the free side of the counter, cleavage showing, and winks at me.

The two guys behind her laugh, one of them slapping her ass. She spins on him, shaking her finger before rolling her eyes at me.

"Can I help you?" I feel suddenly shy at her familiarity, the way she leans in again, bangles singing against the glass counter, dark eyes huge and framed in the thickest lashes I've ever seen. Tiny gold sparkles glitter on the outside edges of her wide eyes, her generous mouth slick with gloss. The little denim jacket cuts off at her ribcage, a flowing yellow dress beneath.

"Of course you can," she says in a voice like butter and velvet poured over spiced chocolate. Winks again. "Though I have a feeling, as sad as it makes me, you're not my type."

My flush returns. Did she just hit on me? She laughs, a rich and engaging sound and I laugh too, unable to stop the nervous giggle escaping. I've never met anyone so charismatic in my life.

"Girlfriend," one of the guys, a gorgeous Hispanic almost too pretty for his own good, says in a softly effeminate voice, "you tell her she's wasting her time."

His companion, lithe and skinny, black hair slicked, eyes dark with liner, cocks one hip and hums a tune in a clear, crisp voice, vocal training obvious to my ears. "I think there's a show tune in there, sugar."

The pair of them break into an improvised song, snapping their fingers and dancing in place while the stunning girl laughs at them and joins them in her deep contralto voice.

I look up. He's watching me. Their friend. The one I noticed first.

The kind, open smile on his face makes me shiver and look away. And think Ian's name over and over like a mantra. One handsome face and I'm forgetting him already? What kind of girlfriend am I?

And then I remember. Ian's dead. He's been dead for a year.

It hits me like a blow.

"Now, then," the girl leans toward me on one elbow, obviously unaware I'm falling apart inside, as her two friends wrap up their song. "Our real reason for being."

"Can anyone ever know their real reason?" Handsome finally speaks, breaks my loop of self-hate and the need to sob over Ian despite the fact I know—I've known for ages—my love is gone. This delicious stranger distracts me with his words. I thought her voice was melodic. His strokes my ears with heat and softness, also trained and trained well. "For being, I mean?"

The girl turns on him, shrugs. "In this instance," she says, radiating so much confidence I wish I could be like her in a stab of sudden envy. "We do." Spins back to me, chin dropping, arms opening. "We require a bouquet, fair maid. But not just any bouquet." The two behind her hum in harmony, back dropping her little performance. "A bouquet to rival all that came before. To stun and amaze in its beauty and grace." Her voice alters from its deep pitch to a softer, higher tone full of angst and sorrow. "Precious flowers to give their lives so that we," she pats her chest with both hands while her choir modulates their hum, "might show our undying love and faithfulness to one we would honor with their deaths."

Her two friends immediately clap as she bows her head, smiling at their false patter of applause. While handsome laughs at them. Turns back to me from his casual observation.

"Just a dozen roses, please," he says.

His two friends—Backup #1and Backup#2— swoon.

"Just!" They say together.

The black girl stomps her foot, but she's grinning behind her scowl. "Such a cruel way to crush the heart of a performer," she says.

He hands over a credit card before I can turn to fill the order, heart pounding, lost in the need to keep listening, the longing to be like them, to join them in their easy way with each other. "Aleah," he says, giving her talent a name, "I have no fear for your heart." He shrugs at me. "Just," stresses it, "the roses. And I'll do my best to keep my companions from scaring off your customers while we wait."

My lips twitch in a grin even as I whisper, "It's okay," and spin away. Realize I still have his credit card in my hand. I slip it into my apron, rush to the refrigerated case. Aunt Vonda, back behind her arrangement, catches my eye.

Grins and leaves me to them.

They must be actors. I'm shivering with excitement, cursing my sudden shyness, wishing I could blurt out I want to be like them even as I look up.

And see Ian's reflection in the glass. He's smiling at me. Is this what he wants? For me to be like them? I hope so.

I really hope so.

My hands fumble in the bucket full of blooms as I wander over the roses, carefully selecting the very best and arrange them in the plastic sleeve, hands shaking.

Try to slow my pounding heart. *Why am I acting like a little kid? They are just people.* I have to remind myself. But I'm still in awe, and, as I staple the paper over the deep, red roses, almost puncturing my index finger in the process, the jab of pain tells me why.

Mom. They act like Mom. She was huge to me despite her slim body. With a towering personality, extravagant with her love and in her manner, always on, always an actress. Boisterous and confident like the girl, Aleah. Full of charisma, filling a room with her presence wherever she went. Like Ian did, despite his illness.

I crave such a life. To be just like Mom. Like Ian. But as I carry the wrapped bouquet to the counter, thinking about my mother and the time we spent together, I feel myself sigh.

*Who am I kidding? I'm not my mother.* And no matter the plays I did, the roles I filled, Ian was always the star.

I set the flowers down, feeling my nerves finally calm. Mom took the time when I was little to teach me what she knew. We spent hours acting out scenes she made up for me, at least when she was home. Her career was in film and on stage, but she insisted I learn, and seemed to love to teach me. I absorbed every bit I could, and adored it. I thought I lost all of that when she died, Dad's disapproval quashing my acting passion. And even though I struck out into acting again in high school, it never felt the same without Mom there to guide me.

Standing here, with the girl Aleah and her friends still messing around, their clear love of the craft pouring out of them, I feel like that part of me has awoken all over again, the dream a sudden reality presented to me in stark relief. And I'm a starving woman who finally found a banquet.

*Acting classes. No more thinking, planning, imagining. I have to start acting classes, now.*

My eyes meet crystal blue and I freeze again. Hold my breath. He smiles, looks down at my waist.

"I'd love to pay," he says. "But you seem to be attached to my card."

How can I be so stupid? I've spent too much time in my own head lately. Not enough focusing on the real world. I fumble in my pocket, red all over again and knowing I've made a fool of myself even while I wonder what it is about him that makes me care. That drives Ian to the back of my mind when he's dominated it for so long.

I fish out the card and, with hands that won't stop shaking, ring in the flowers.

When I hand back his card, his fingers brush mine and he smiles again, gentle and kind. "I see you have a copy of *Backstage*," he says. I spin, eyes wide, mortified the magazine is making things worse though I'm not sure why they are worse. "Are you an actress?"

I choke on my tongue before I'm able to speak. "My mother was," I say as Aleah and her two buddies lean in. Draw a breath. "And I've done some. Just local stuff. Back home."

I'm a lame duck, fatally injured and wish someone would just come and put me out of my misery. Can I possibly sound more pathetic to their obviously cultured ears? But he nods like he understands, Aleah smiling brighter.

"Not sure if you're in classes or not," he says, casual, as though it's no big deal to him even as my heart feels like it's going to leap out of my chest. "But there's a great one we all go to every other night. If you're interested."

Aleah bounces on her toes, nodding. "Yes, please come." She jerks her thumb at the two behind her. "We need more women, and queens don't count."

This time I really choke. Have to cough a few times to clear my throat. Sure, I have a few friends back home who are gay. But no one really talks about it in the open. And I've always been sensitive about labels.

The pair fake shock, spin on their heels and march out while Aleah laughs and goes after them with a wave goodbye and a blown kiss. I watch her go, wishing I could follow.

Lock eyes with handsome who waits, patient and silent.

For what? I gave him his card, his flowers.

Dear God. His question.

"Sure." The word erupts out of me.

He leans in, the scent of coffee and something sweet carrying with him as he reaches for a pen. Takes my hand. I can barely feel the tickle of the nib as he writes down an address and a name on my palm. I'm too distracted by the fact he's touching me.

The click of the pen retracting under his thumb breaks me out of a trance created by the warmth of his strong fingers. I miss his touch when he steps back, lifting the bouquet into his arms.

"Tomorrow night," he says. "See you then."

I wave, a half-hearted and measly attempt at a goodbye, as he turns and leaves. My eyes descend from the back of his head to the pull of his shoulders inside his t-shirt. How his stature seems wide despite his leanness.

How the rear pockets of his jeans do a great job showing off his—

The doorbell jingles and he's gone out the storefront into the sunlight. He and his friends walk past the window, smiling, laughing, a silent film of joy I long for with so much sudden need my hands clench around the edge of the counter to keep me in place.

I thought the best part of dreaming was imagining how things could be. Now I know better.

I was so wrong. I know what perfect looks like. And I want it for myself.

# Chapter Four

My heart is thudding so loud I'm sure everyone can hear it as I walk down the street with confidence I don't feel toward the address I carefully copied from my sweaty palm the afternoon before. Aunt Vonda pounced almost immediately after the foursome left the shop, beaming and bouncy.

"He was so cute," she breathed before giggling like a girl. "And his friends seemed fun."

I loved her so much right then, more than I ever thought possible, as I giggled back. I would never have been able to have this nervously excited moment with anyone else.

She grabbed my hand, read the address before looking up into my eyes, her green ones hopeful. "You're going to go?"

*Why else have I been combing through* Backstage *the last three days?* Despite my growing nervousness as I thought about it, I nodded, decision made. I wanted to be like them so badly. I felt bits and pieces of what Aleah and her friends exuded during my stints in school plays and small community theater productions I'd used as an escape from Ian's illness. The only escape I allowed myself because he loved to see me perform.

"I'm going to go." She turned away, satisfied, still chattering about how amazing it was going to be and I was already a wonderful actress, she loved me in my last play. Meanwhile, I read the name below the address.

Miller. Was that the teacher? I ran to the register and checked his slip with trembling fingers. Handsome's name is Miller Hill.

The perfect name for an actor.

I spent the whole night at home suffering a case of nerves even as guilt about my attraction to Miller fought with memories of Ian. I missed him, my lost love. He didn't appear all night, not lying on my bed with his crooked smile, not whispering in my ear. It made me sad, worried he'd gone. I finally forced myself to stop, relax.

Ian would always be with me. As for this silly attraction to a guy I just met... I wasn't going to sleep with him or anything. I was going to an acting class.

I stared at my reflection in the mirror and had a pep talk with myself for once.

"You, Miss Riley James," I poked a finger at myself, doing my best Ian impersonation, "are a grown woman. With a backbone. Find it already."

So there.

Work the next day alternately dragged and flew by, Aunt Vonda finally shooing me off an hour before the class was supposed to start.

"Go make yourself pretty," she'd said. While I blushed all over again.

And now, not even sixty minutes later, I'm walking down the street, heading for the address Miller gave me. Doing my best not to turn and throw up.

The only thing keeping me from public puking is

the fact Ian is back. Smiling down at me as he strides along beside me, his memory passing through strangers, the fantasy of his presence enough to keep me moving.

I cross at a green light, past a silver car, spotting the street I'm looking for marked clearly on the sign above. The driver revs his engine, the thumping sound of heavy bass emerging from inside, windows blacked out. I hurry, hating the trickle of fear spreading through me as the phantom of Ian gives the driver the finger and laughs.

I will not be afraid, not of anything. Not while he's beside me.

(We) pause on the corner, just to breathe. Up ahead, a handful of people walk up some steps and into a building. The glass doorway flashes in the failing light, the number written clearly across it, reflected back. The one I'm looking for.

My destination is a blunt little building with a crumbling front foundation, the stairs pitted, the railing rusty. But the door looks clean. I double check the number against the piece of paper in my hand. This is the place.

I'm here. I'm really doing this.

My feet won't move though I'm telling them to. And then I'm not doing this after all, I'm half-turning to leave, mouth dry, chest tight. It's so much easier to just imagine I'm an actor, to dream about it. The doing, not so much.

*Trust me, Rye*, Ian whispers in my memory. *You'll be fantastic*.

My breathing is shaky, but I'm spinning back. My legs move, carrying me forward while Ian's imagined presence keeps urging me on. Up the stairs, the rail gritty under my hand. The door sighs with cool air rushing at me as I pull it open and enter the small foyer.

Musty disuse hits me in the face, mixed with the faint scent of urine. But a hand-written sign says "ACTING CLASS TONIGHT" and an equally wavering arrow points up the narrow stairs.

Ian drifts past me, pauses to look down. *Coming?*

I take the first step, boots crunching over debris, hand clutching reflexively around the railing as I walk through his ghost and up the flight. My fingers trace across the paint on the other wall, for balance. To keep me connected to the world. It's not until I reach the second floor I realize I'm probably going to want to wash my hands now.

And maybe throw up for real. Instead, I force my feet to move, my lungs to breathe, and stuff my hands in my pockets as I walk down the hall under the flickering bulb of the main light. The ceiling arches high overhead. A shame, someone painted the period trim and crown moldings a hideous brown, the industrial tile floor adding an air of dingy, trying-to-be chic. The scent of mustiness is reduced up here, though I can smell other things that make me wince.

I keep my focus on the open door ahead, a second sign hanging from the frosted glass. And Ian appearing again, beckoning for me to walk through. I think about running. What kind of class is this in a place bums likely used for a toilet?

*Trust me*, Ian says again.

And I do, even as I doubt my sanity.

It's too late to retreat, in any case. I'm at the door, peeking in. I see Aleah just before she spots me and shrieks.

"Flower girl!" She's circling the rickety desk and throwing herself at me before I can back away, hugging me around the neck. Her body feels hot and hard, hair coarse on my skin, lips wet when she kisses my cheek before smacking my shoulder with one hand. "I really didn't think you'd come."

I can barely muster a smile despite the fact my insides are now singing. I have to shake this off, drop the need to bolt. I've never been shy. I refuse to let this weirdness tugging on me, begging me to leave, to drag me out when I know I'm in the right place.

At last. Ian smiles over Aleah's shoulder before fading away.

"It sounded like fun," I say. Wanting to tell her the reason I'm here is because of her and her funny friends. Because Miller invited me.

And because Ian believes in me still.

"Girl," she retreats around her table again, opens a cashbox, "you have no idea. Ten bucks for your first session. You like it, there's a monthly sign up."

I hand over my money, needing my smile to be confident, yet knowing it's more church mouse than charismatic. "Thank you."

Aleah grabs my arm even as she stands on her tiptoes. I finally look into the room, a ring of mismatched chairs around the outside, leaving the center empty. No, not empty. Full of people.

Other actors. Real ones.

I'm going to be sick.

"There's Piper," she points as though she has no idea I'm so nervous I feel like I'm going to leave what little I managed to eat on her lovely shoes. And I hope she doesn't notice. I follow her finger with my gaze, see one of the guys she was with earlier, the Goth one. "And Ruben." Her Hispanic friend stands beside Piper. "Go hang out with them until I'm done here."

I nod to her, step away as she turns to greet someone at the door. Freeze up.

I can't do this. But I have to. Aleah is right behind me and I have a feeling she won't let me leave.

Someone touches my shoulder and I turn with a

gasp, expecting Ian.

My gaze meets blue eyes so clear they sparkle.

"Nice to see you made it," Miller says.

*Say something. Just open your stupid mouth and say some —*

"Hi," I say, while inside I roll my eyes and groan, "Miller." I've never felt so awkward in my life.

"Hi, yourself," he says, shrugging out of a jacket he tosses onto the nearest chair at the back wall. He holds out his hand and I shake it. "You know my name," he says at last.

"Riley." At least my voice isn't shaking. Much. "Riley James."

He grins, releases my hand. "Nice to meet you, Riley James."

I survived the introduction. And I'm walking with Miller, toward Piper and Ruben who finally spot me and squeal at the top of their lungs, bouncing up and down in place until I'm beside them, and they are hugging me.

Like I'm some long-lost friend.

"Oh, pumpkin," Ruben says, tsking as he looks at my boots. "Those are so last year."

I'm hurt, even though I know he doesn't mean anything by it. But I love my boots. Piper pushes Ruben out of the way. "I adore them," he says. "Don't mind the bitch, here." He thumbs over his shoulder at his friend. "She's such a diva."

I laugh before I can stop myself.

And relax all of a sudden. This was the right decision. And I'm very glad I'm here.

A tall, older man in a scruffy t-shirt, long hair hanging behind him in a ponytail, strides into the room. Everyone turns to face him, some of the young actors rushing to his side. I catch one of them watching me. I'm stunned by how beautiful she is. Flawless skin, flowing blonde hair, perfect figure, statuesque. She should be in movies.

From the way she turns from me, arrogant nose in the air, she probably thinks so, too.

It's difficult not to feel intimidated. I allow a single *bitch* to roll around in my head before Aleah slams the door shut and runs to join us.

"Welcome, students." The man might look scruffy, at least twice our age if not older, but he has the voice of an actor and a singer. "Those of you who know me, you'll be bored by my introduction to those who don't." Laughter, though almost canned, as if this is an old joke. So he's a comedian. I think I can handle that, feel myself relax further. "I am Roger Osmore, lord of stage and screen. And I am your teacher."

His lordship's name isn't familiar, so I make a mental note to Google him later.

Roger launches directly into a lecture as the class spreads out, some taking the chairs against the walls, some sitting on the floor at his feet. I listen, or at least try. But with every word he speaks, Mom's past words come shining through.

"Good acting is about sinking into the role," Roger says, while Mom's voice whispers, *We aren't actors, Rye. We channel to a higher power. To another state of mind. If you can find the place where you don't exist, where you are only the character you portray, you have found heaven.*

I'd found that place before, the one she talked about. Mom called it pure creation energy, like being the center of the Universe. It was easier when I was a little girl, my imagination huge and open. When Mom died, I lost my desire to act because I missed her so much. Not to mention Dad's disapproval of all things Riley. But when the chance came to audition for the school production of *Romeo and Juliet*, Ian insisted. He knew all about my passion when I was little. He knew everything about me.

I signed up to make him happy, never expecting to get the part. Spent that night whispering with him, how fabulous it was, confessing my dream to be just like my mother, a dream I'd given up long ago. I spent months in rehearsals, split between learning my part and Ian, despite Dad's loud protests.

And, the first night of the production, nerves jangling, I finally found the quiet place Mom told me about all over again.

I was hooked after that, craving the escape into stillness while falling into the brilliant beauty of being the source of a character's voice. Thrilling, to emerge from it to applause and beaming smiles, to be praised, to hear I was talented.

Who wouldn't love that?

But the best part was always Ian's smile, his enthusiasm no matter how he felt. Whether in a wheelchair or able to sit in one of the regular seats, he never missed a show.

Until the last performance of the final production I took part in, just a little over a year ago. When I came out of my character and returned to the real world, he was gone. His parents gone with him.

And I knew I'd never act again as long as he lived. Which wasn't long. He'd relapsed, badly, the cancer racing through him this time where once it had taken a more sedate pace. Devouring him from the inside out, at a speed no transfusions or bone marrow treatments could halt.

Two weeks later he died. And despite my promise to pursue my dream to be an actor, I hadn't. Until this moment.

*Am I really doing it?*

Someone jabs me in the ribs and I start, releasing a meep of shock. Aleah tilts her head, makes a face and I suddenly realize everyone is staring. Including Roger.

"Well?" He glares like I'm wasting his time. "Do you own a tongue? If not, the mime class is down the hall in about, oh, never."

Everyone laughs. Even Aleah, though she looks sorry she did. I glance at Miller, afraid I've embarrassed him, let him down.

Not everyone is laughing. He looks irritated. *Shit.*

"Can you repeat the question?" I'm in high school and he's a bully teacher making me feel like I'm a smear under his shoe. Roger scowls deeper.

"In my class," he draws the words out, "I expect you to pay attention. I do not," he sniffed, "repeat myself."

More titters from the class, though now I'm pissed off. I like this better. I can handle angry. Considering I'm paying him and not the other way around, he can damned well drop the arrogance act.

"Good to know," I say before I can stop myself. "When you get to the part that interests me, I'm happy to answer."

It takes me a moment to inhale past my own shock. I hate being cornered and pushed around, always have. Roger no longer reminds me of a bully teacher.

With his face all scrunched and disapproving, he reminds me of my dad.

More laughter, but this time, the joke's on him. His jaw clenches. I know he's going to kick me out. Sharp regret pangs in my chest. But I accept it.

This isn't the place for me. But I'll find it.

I will.

To my surprise, Roger turns away, starting up his lecture again. I feel someone touch my hand, look over and up at Miller.

Who's laughing silently. Winks at me.

And I smile back.

Maybe it is my place after all.

# *Chapter Five*

The lecture doesn't last long, Roger quickly moving on to splitting us into groups. I leave Aleah and Miller behind, though I'm assigned to the same one as Piper, so at least I know someone. I'm nervous, feel my hands quivering, butterflies dancing around in my stomach. The others are watching me, I just know it. And I'm gripped by the realization I'm going to make an ass of myself.

Two of the actors step into the center, launch into an improvised scene. I barely see or hear them, ready to back away and leave. As I begin to turn, I meet Piper's eyes.

He's smiling at me, handsome face twisting sideways in a grin, hip cocked in the same direction, chin tucked as he leans toward me. We're about the same height, making it easy for him to hover his face close to mine. I see his thick lashes, the dark line of his makeup, the sparkle in his pale green eyes.

"Riley," he drags my name out so it sounds like "Ryyyyyley." "Sweetie." Same draw on the vowel. "You're awesome."

I don't know what to say, just stare, though I can feel my butterflies retreating.

"Listen," he says, ignoring the world around us, waving one finger under my nose, "don't you ever let anyone tell you otherwise. Even if you stink." He tosses his head, sniffs. "Even if you are the worst actor on the face of this planet," Piper meets my eyes again. "You." He pokes me gently in the chest. "Are." Again with the poke, followed by a soft cheek pinch. "Awesome."

I gulp down a rising lump in my throat and manage a smile. "Thank you."

Piper's grin widens before he spins with perfect timing. The center is empty. His hand hooks my arm and, all of a sudden, I'm in the middle. With him. His bubbly persona fades as he hunches his shoulders, lower jaw jutting, lips curved as though he's toothless. My new friend is no longer a lean Goth, but a little old man with a cranky disposition.

I see it clearly, as though the character has been drawn over Piper. And instantly sync my own physique, calling up an old lady.

I don't remember what we said, how the scene resolved. I only remember returning to the outside of the circle to applause and laughter where Piper hugs me with great enthusiasm.

"You don't stink," he says.

"You either," I say.

The next two hours fly by in a mix of awe and excitement, laughter and the elusive pull of the quiet place. I feel the edges of it, calling me as I become braver, not only at Piper's side anymore, engaging total strangers alone in the center or, in the end, stepping out myself.

I know I'm so close, falling into the perfect mental space, when Roger interrupts.

"And that," he says while I stare dumbly, drained but invigorated at the same time, "is class."

Everyone applauds, myself included, though not for the teacher. For the experience. The weak and weary feeling retreats, replaced by a sense of rightness I embrace with my whole heart.

Piper hugs me again. "You were mahvelous."

I laugh, breathless and happy. "Piper," I say, "you're so talented." I'm amazed how much of a chameleon he's been in the last two hours. From innocent little girl to action hero to quiet priest all the way to an opera singer belting out an aria, Piper has shown me what I'm lacking.

He bows to me before straightening and offering a cutesy curtsy. "I'd like to thank all the little people."

Ruben calls his name from across the room, breaking up our party. "I will see you," Piper says, backing away with a suggestive toss of his hips, "later."

I wave, sigh in contentment, already thinking of him as a friend. I realize then all the others are drifting toward the door. Aleah is head-down with the gorgeous blonde girl who hasn't looked my way since her earlier arrogant stare. I can't spot Miller, but and Ruben skip toward the exit, singing. I grin and move after them.

"New girl," Roger's voice breaks my happy and turns me around. "A moment."

*Shit. He's going to yell at me now.* I tense inside. I hate confrontations. Especially now I've connected this teacher with Dad. But as I approach, wary and ready to say screw it and leave, he smiles. Like by doing so he's granting me some kind of favor.

"I don't like being challenged," he says. "But, I do appreciate spunk." Up close, I can see how he could have been a leading man, once. In the structure of his jaw and cheekbones, the depth of his dark eyes. He's tall, as big as my father, but unlike my firefighter dad, Roger has gone soft, belly protruding just a little under his tattered sweater. And his jowls have begun to sag, giving desperation to his attempt at being hip and staying young. The faint line of gray hair at his scalp proves I'm right.

I can't imagine my father dyeing his hair. It's just odd.

"Okay," I say, about to turn away when Roger closes the space between us, hand reaching out to my arm, to stop me.

Lingering there until the discomfort grows so heavy I clear my throat as he speaks.

"You have talent," he says, voice deep. Is he trying to be sexy? I'm dying inside, partly from laughter, partly from revulsion. "I have an eye for it."

"Great," I say, out of words, needing to just run, but I can't. It's as if I'm held in thrall by the touch of his hand on my arm. Sliding down over my elbow to grip it. Still holding me in one place. I'm sure he thinks it's his charm and dashing good looks.

Truthfully, I feel so horrified I can't move.

"I'd like to offer you some free classes," he says. Leans closer, close enough I smell the foul mix of cheap aftershave and alcohol, see the stubble he missed shaving, catch the cracks in his teeth, etched with coffee stains. "You can be a star."

I hover on the edge of kicking him in the nuts and bolting when an arm slides around my shoulders, easing me free of Roger's grip. I look up and see Miller, now hugging me against his side, hip pressed to my waist, smiling at the teacher.

I'm so absorbed in the warmth of his touch, the suddenness of Miller's embrace, I almost miss the fact he's not "nice" smiling. More like "touch her again and I'll kill you" smiling. It makes me giggle just a little. I smother it with my hand as Miller casually turns to me.

"We're late," he says. "As fun as this has been, we should hurry, yeah?"

I nod, eyes flickering to Roger. I didn't need to be rescued. I really didn't. But it's nice, for a change, to be the one taken care of.

Roger doesn't say anything, just watches us leave as Miller pauses only to scoop up his jacket and my purse. His arm slides from around my shoulders, fingers connecting with mine, leading me out by the hand. I'm lost in the sensation of his touch. I still feel his arm around me, the heat of his body. I shiver.

He must take it as a rejection, releasing my hand as we run down the stairs to the exit. I exhale into the night air, draw a breath and laugh. And Miller laughs with me.

Aleah looks up from where she waits on the corner, head tilted, smiling. "Share!"

I shake my head, turn to Miller. "Thanks," I say.

"Roger's an ass," he says. "I'm sorry, I should have warned you. But it's a great group, right?"

I smile, nod. Roger forgotten, my father. Even Ian, for a moment. I hug myself and turn in a circle, knowing I look like a fool before I see Aleah repeat my act. I'm wrong. Not a fool.

I look like I belong. Like I'm an actor.

Miller walks down the steps with me, our feet in time on the treads. He laughs as we exaggerate the motion, finally tromping our way, one measured step at a time, to Aleah. She shakes her head, twists her lips in a "hell no, you did not just act like three-year-olds" kind of way.

"If you two are done," she says. "We have places to be. And shit to do."

Miller grabs her around the waist, kisses her cheek noisily, blowing a raspberry at the end. "Yes, Momma Bear," he says.

She swats him, giggles. Turns to me. "Makes a sister think about trading teams." She hums a soft tune of approval. "You better watch this boy," she says. "Or he'll make you fall in love with his fine, white ass."

Why does that hit me so hard? The word "love" breaks my joy, the moment, shatters it. I'm cold all of a sudden, though the night is anything but. I back away a step even as Miller frowns, concern on his face.

With no idea Ian hovers behind him, looking sad and lost. Like I've broken his heart.

"We're going for coffee," Miller says, holds out his hand. Ian doesn't move, his phantom staring at me with his hurt hazel eyes. I barely hear Miller as he goes on. "Kind of tradition."

It's terrible standing there, seeing two where there's really only one. It's worse that I want to grab hold of Miller, forget I already gave my heart and lost the love of my life, now hovering and watching as I betray him with a stranger.

I can't go through with it, not with Ian's sad eyes burning through my soul. As much as it would be brilliant.

I just can't.

Miller must see it in my face because he lets his hand drop. Even Aleah suddenly looks upset.

"Riley Skyley," she says, singing my name. "Don't make me drag you."

I'm already out of her reach, backing up, tripping over a garbage bag on the side of the street. Ian still stares though I refuse to look over Miller's shoulder, to see the guilt I've manifested in the fake image of my dead boyfriend. "I have to go." Running is the only solution. Because I have nothing else to offer as an excuse.

I raise my hand in farewell, feeling the need to do something to wipe the look of disappointment from

Miller's face. "Thank you!"

Like a coward, I turn and sprint for home while Ian trails behind me.

I keep my head down, thoughts spinning. *This is wrong, I can't just move on. I barely know Miller. And it's clear Ian doesn't want me to. Wait, that's crazy.* I pant out a breath through my mouth. *This figment of my imagination doesn't control what I do. That's even crazier.*

Reality. I need to ground myself in the real world for this logic to work. *What the hell is going on with my hormones some cute guy can make me spin out of control like this?* That's better, clearer, less nuts. I feel Ian is still with me. I know I'm probably totally loony by now. And yet, Miller seems to be able to lift me out of my memories of Ian.

Can I just abandon them like my boyfriend never existed?

And what kind of person does that make me?

I pause at a red light, halfway home, gulping air as I realize that's the real problem. I don't want to forget Ian. I don't want to stop seeing him everywhere, hearing his whispered voice, feeling his presence when I lose myself in my imagination. If I do move on, if I let myself even consider what might or might not happen with Miller—or any other guy—I'm afraid I'll forget. That Ian will fade from me faster than he already is. I hate admitting I struggle to remember what his voice sounds like. Why I really only hear him whisper, now. Needing to listen to the few videos I have of him, ones we made on purpose, just so I could see him again. I clung to one of his t-shirts for weeks after he died, but his scent didn't last, fading too fast.

The light turns green. Someone jostles me from behind on the way by as I stay still, rooted in my fear and sadness, mind churning. *But I'm going to have to let go of him someday, right? I can't live like this. He told me over and over, until I begged him to stop. He wanted me to be happy, to find love again.*

And yet I'm clinging to his memory every day, calling him up so I don't have to be alone.

I shiver, angry with myself, even as Ian's voice murmurs in my head.

*Love you*, he says.

I start walking again, shoulders squared. *Stupid, of course I'll move on. But not now, not yet. It's too soon. Someday, okay.*

*Just not today.*

I pass Ian's shade at the corner, still watching me with hurt in his eyes, trying not to feel sad about choosing his ghost over Miller.

# Chapter Six

I feel Aunt Vonda's eyes on me all morning. She hasn't said a word yet, she must be waiting for me to comment about last night. It's cruel of me not to say anything, but I really don't know what to say.

She finally broaches the topic over our quick lunch, hunched in the tiny staff room out back while I watch the empty front, one foot holding the door open.

"How was class?" She rushes on as though expecting a negative response. "I'm sure it's always hard the first time and all. Everyone has to start somewhere." Aunt Vonda stumbles to a halt, setting aside her sandwich and sighing over her bottle of water. "Was it awful?"

"It was wonderful," I say, smiling then, thinking of Piper and his pep talk.

Aunt Vonda beams before frowning. "I thought when you didn't say anything—"

I reach for her hand and squeeze it, the skin soft, her many gold rings digging into her flesh from years of wear. "I'm sorry," I say. "I didn't mean to keep you in the dark. It really was a lot of fun. I guess I'm just trying to decide if I want to go back."

The startled look she gives me makes me giggle. "Of course you're going back," she says. "Why wouldn't you?"

How can I tell her about my fear of leaving Ian behind? Of his sad face as I curled up last night, the soft sigh I felt against my cheek as I closed my eyes to sleep? I know what she'll say—beyond the obvious "you need a therapist and drugs."

That Ian's already gone.

I shrug instead, pick at my salad without trace of an appetite, wondering if I really wish it were true. That I could stop conjuring his memory into my own version of life. "It just seems silly, now," I say. Not meaning it at all. There was nothing silly about last night. "The teacher was a bit of a jerk." That much is true. "Maybe I'll look into going to acting school instead of college."

There, I said it out loud before my fear could stop me. Knowing Dad will have a fit. He wants me to be a teacher or a nurse or something "useful". He made it clear when I started acting in school and community theater, it was only a phase I was going through and I'd be moving on to a real career.

Aunt Vonda's little smile tells me she's not going to give me the same lecture. "I think it's a great idea, pet," she says.

So do I. And, finally smiling again, so does Ian where he stands, shoulder against the wall, watching me.

"You just promise me one thing." Aunt Vonda sets aside her sandwich, leaning toward me over the narrow table. "You won't ever let life knock you down. You'll get back up and keep going. Because you're the only one who matters."

She must think I'm focused on Dad, not the fuzzy image of Ian I've made up in my head. I smile and nod and continue to poke at my salad.

The bell rings, but before I can get up, Aunt

Vonda rushes past me with a soft pat to my shoulder, her body barreling through Ian's shade, breaking apart my illusion. She leaves me to brood and try to make him come back, to reform the fantasy even as last night's memories do their best to win out over his fading ones.

*So what am I brooding over, exactly? What is my problem? I had a brilliant time last night, met some actors just like me. Actually held my own, if I do say so myself. It was incredible and I'm sitting here like someone pulled my pigtails and called me names while I mope over the fact I had so much fun I can't hide in my imaginary boyfriend anymore.*

I think of Piper and his fabulous ability. Of Aleah and Ruben. All the talented actors I met last night. I do my best not to think of Miller, though he appears in my mind more often than anyone else. Superimposing himself over Ian. And I shake myself loose of my melancholy.

I'm being an asshole. Now that I'm no longer moping, I smile into my greens, feeling a tingle of happiness race through me. *Just because I'm having a little trouble keeping Ian front and center doesn't mean I don't love him anymore. And it's probably good for me to live a little.* Besides, I still have our private moments. But the thought of having a life to live is nice, and I know the real Ian—not the construct I've use to guilt myself into hiding for the last year— would never want me to hold back.

Next class isn't until Monday, but that's okay. It gives me lots of time to work on my own. To dig out some of my old monologues, Google some more. Research theater schools here in New York.

And just like that, my path unwinds before me. I shiver a little, knowing Ian isn't at the end of it. But I'm excited to think I just might be able to make this work.

As for Miller... I can be his friend. That

understanding makes me grin. *God, I'm such a freak. Of course. Friends, how perfect.* I can hang out with him and not date him or anything. If he's okay with that. And if he's not, I'll find some other actors to befriend and spend time with. I don't have to be afraid to lose Ian. Nothing—no one—will ever take him away from me.

His fantasy smiles at me as I dump the remains of my lunch and go back to work.

I help Aunt Vonda close up shop that night in a much better mood. We link arms for the walk home as I chatter to her about the three schools I've been reading about in *Backstage*. We're bouncy and giggling by the time we arrive at the apartment.

I leave her to her favorite cop show on TV and go up to the rooftop with the trade magazine and my laptop. It's a warm night, but not humid, perfect for looking out over the city, practicing characters, singing some show tunes I find on YouTube.

Ian's shade perches on the edge of the rooftop ledge, feet kicking like he loved to do, shoulders hunched forward, sweet smile on his face. Maybe I should feel lonely, being by myself up there on a Friday night. But I don't. I'm so wrapped up in what I'm doing, I barely notice time passing, performing for the make-believe Ian I've perfected. When I look up from a study on Shakespeare and modern theater, to tell him how cool this is, it's almost midnight.

Someone sings below me. I set down my computer and lean over the edge of the roof wall, looking down at the street. A small group of people are walking by. No, dancing by, laughing and talking and singing in harmony snatches of song.

It makes my heart ache to run down and join them, to be part of what they have. I think of my new acting friends and how, if I'd not been such a loser last night, I could have found a taste of the magic walking by my apartment building.

They are gone far too soon, three guys, three girls, their voices mingling like heaven's choir when they sing, laughter almost as beautiful. I heave a huge sigh when I finally stand back, the last echoes of their street party fading away.

Ian is still smiling at me.

I'm crying all of a sudden, my heart crushing into a tiny ball of hurt so powerful I can barely breathe. I used to experience these moments, but haven't had one for months. Way worse than my cry in the car on my way out of Clifton. Debilitating, crushing, the black pit of despair sucking me in. I'm aware of my aloneness then, of being one half of a whole that will never be again, our harmony— mine and Ian's—dead with him as his image just watches me.

It's terrible, and I feel guilt even as I dial, but I have to talk to someone. And I can only think of one person who will understand.

Susan answers on the first ring. From the coarseness of her voice, I'm not the only one who's been crying. Hearing the thickness when she says, "Rye," makes me burst into tears. I hear her sobbing on the other end and cling to the phone as I sink with my back against the roof wall, next to Ian's shadow, gravel digging into my skin through my jeans as I hug my knees to my chest. I feel him sink down next to me as I weep and grind my teeth and try not to fall into the despair I've embraced so many times in the last year.

We've done this before, Susan and me, but not for a while. When Ian first found out his cancer was back, I called his mother and heard her crying. Cried with her. Since then, any time one of us felt like bawling, we called.

I just wish I had the courage to tell her I keep him with me just in case she didn't answer the phone.

It's a long time before either of us speaks. Susan manages first. "Oh, Rye," she hiccups softly before drawing a shaking breath that hisses over the line. "Are you okay?"

"Are you?" I kick at some gravel with the toe of my sneaker. "You were crying before I called."

She's quiet a long moment. "Just going through some old things," she says. "Trying to sort out the last of Ian's stuff to send to charity."

Damn it, I was going to help her do that before I left. "I'm sorry," I start to say, but she cuts me off.

"Don't you even," she says with a laugh through the last of her tears. "You've done enough. Now, tell me how New York is so I can live vicariously."

I almost don't tell her about acting, even as Ian whispers at me to share everything. But Susan has been a mother to me since my own died, my best friend's—and then boyfriend's—amazing mom. I spill about the class, skim over Miller, focus on how cool it was.

When I ramble to a halt, Susan's excitement is clear when she answers.

"You have to tell us when you're doing a show," she says. "We want to be there."

I hear Dwight's voice agree with enthusiasm in the background, know he's up with her, at least, someone to hug her and take care of her now that our cry is over. A real person, not a shadow like I have.

It's the first time I wish I'd let Ian go in favor of a flesh and blood someone and wince at my betrayal.

"I will," I say. "Thanks. For being here for me."

Susan chokes even as I feel my chest tighten all over again.

"We will always be here for you," she says, voice loud and distorted. I picture her lips very close to the phone, probably clutching it with both hands. "Always."

I say goodbye, hugs for Dwight. Hang up and lean my head back, dropping my phone into my lap as I let my legs stretch out across the graveled surface of the roof.

School is a yes. I love acting too much not to give it a try. I'll spend the summer figuring out what I want, making money. Apply when I know which one I want to attend and keep my fingers crossed for the winter semester.

Meanwhile, I'm going to need more experience. And though I could go to another class, I like the people I've met in this one.

I wipe at my tears, stand and retrieve my laptop. Pause to see Ian's left me alone on the roof.

That I've left myself alone.

I think I'm finally done with that.

# Chapter Seven

I'm crossing the street, eyes locked on my destination so narrowly, I bump into someone.

"Nice to see you're back," Miller says as he catches me, holds me gently but firmly in his hands.

I blush immediately on the crowded street, tucking close to him to avoid being jostled by passing pedestrians. He guides me aside, close to the corner building, body curved around mine to protect me. It's sweet, but I don't need to be protected.

So why haven't I stepped away yet? Or shrugged off his one hand still resting on my waist?

At least there's no sign of my guilt about standing here with him so close. My imagined Ian is nowhere in sight.

I smile with calm I don't feel. "I had so much fun last time," I say, trying for some sparkle in my voice, mentally wincing and dialing it down when all I hear from my own mouth is fake yuck. "You were right about the class." That feels better, more normal, less hysterically trying to come across as real. "It was great."

Miller lets his hand drop, but his smile remains, warmth in his blue eyes, in the soft frown of his brow as he leans close, intimate but not overpowering, just a private moment in a not-so-private setting. I'm acutely aware of him, how he smells like coffee and sugar, and, peripherally, of the street around us, horns honking, people striding past.

They fade, the whole world does, when Miller speaks.

"Piper said you were brilliant," he says. "And what I saw really impressed me. Who was your mother?"

I gulp down a breath. "My mother?" Oh, yes. Hadn't I told him my mother was an actress? "Marie James," I say. "But she worked under Marie St. Claire." Her maiden name. I think it bothers Dad to this day. Not that I care.

Miller's eyes widen. "No wonder you look familiar," he says. "I adored your mother's work."

He knows Mom? I almost latch onto him in excitement, forgetting my nerves, my shyness, the discomfort of my body's soft yearning for him. The little girl in me is desperate for a connection to my mother beyond the hazy memories I still carry "You watched her movies?" Mom was a "B" actress at best, at least according to her.

But Miller shakes his head. "No, not at first," he says. "I saw her on stage when I was twelve. She was incredible." It's his turn to blush. "I had a huge crush on your mother."

Maybe that should be creepy, but it isn't.

"I went to every show of hers I could," he says, now leaning against the brick with one shoulder, hands in his pockets, smile easy and open. "And when I found out she made movies, I watched those, too." He laughs. "You must think I'm crazy."

Miller doesn't know crazy.

"I never got to see her on stage." Admitting it makes me want to cry, the old pain surfacing as it hasn't in a very long time. "But I rewatch her movies at least once a year."

Miller straightens and bows to me. "You may not know it," he says, "but your mother is a bit of a legend in the theater community. Using her name could open some doors for you."

Now it's my turn to shake my head. "No thanks," I say. "Besides, Mom died a long time ago."

Miller shrugs, offers me his arm. "Your secret is safe with me," he says. "But don't expect it to remain one for long. Especially once you're cast in a show or two."

Good to know. I realize then, beyond seeing her films, I know so little of Mom's life as a performer. *Time to do something about that.*

Miller pauses at the bottom of the stairs to class. His face creases in concern, voice low. "I forgot to mention," he says, "if you have any trouble with Roger tonight, just let me know."

Trouble with—

I sigh. *Roger, right.* And smile at Miller.

"I'll be fine," I say, marching up the steps. "But thanks."

It used to bother me when Ian acted protective, I think because he was so weak and didn't have the energy to waste standing up for me. But I don't seem to have a problem with Miller doing it.

I'm mulling that over when I walk through the door, Miller behind me, to a huge hug from Aleah. She pushes me back, her dark eyes narrowed, huge hoop earrings tossing as she glares.

"You're coming out with us tonight," she says.

I grin. "I am," I say. "Thanks for the order, captain." And salute her.

Aleah laughs, swats my arm. Bats her lashes at

Miller.

Who winks back.

I smell a conspiracy, but don't complain as I hand over my ten dollars and follow Miller to the center of the room, still not sure if I want to pay Roger his full fee or not. I feel more at home tonight, less like the new girl. When I spot the gorgeous blonde woman staring at me again, I stare back until she looks away.

Piper lunges from the crowd, hugs me around the neck so tight I choke.

"Riley," he says. "Where have you been all my life?"

I kiss his cheek, totally outside my comfort zone, but I adore him completely. "Right here, waiting for you."

He gasps, touches the place my lips were, flutters his thick lashes much as Aleah had just done. "Didn't I tell you how incredible you were?"

Ruben snorts, tosses his head at me. Then smiles. "Don't make me jealous, hon."

I hug him, too and he hugs me back. "As if." I look down at his boots. "You need to take me shopping." Yes, I love mine, wearing them right now actually, but his are gorgeous. Chocolate leather with soft black etching and chrome tips.

Ruben slips his arm around my waist. "We'll talk," he says. Eyes my figure. "I can make you look so good."

Piper grabs my arm, pulls me free. "She's already hawtness," he says. "Leave a girl be."

I see Miller watching, laughing, and I have to laugh, too. Even while my cheeks flame with embarrassment. Not from the guys and their banter. But because of the way Miller looks at me.

Or the way I imagine he's looking at me. I shake off my assumptions. *For all I know, he's just being nice.* Even though the soft heat in his blue eyes stirs things in me I forgot were alive and well despite Ian's loss and I find myself wondering what Miller looks like in the dark.

With his clothes off.

I gasp when I realize where my imagination is taking me.

Roger appears, saving me from my overactive fantasy life and near-death from acute embarrassment just for thinking like that.

Another lecture, this one about as interesting as the last. I'm not paying attention, running through the weekend I spent working on my acting and researching techniques, especially improvisational techniques. Roger barely looks at me, doesn't ask me a question this time. Aleah comes to my side, takes my hand when he finally breaks us into groups.

I'm supposed to go off with Ruben's this time, but Aleah has other ideas. She pushes Piper toward his boyfriend and drags me with her. It's not until I'm in the circle I realize Aleah and Miller are both beside me.

Knowing he's here, that I'm going to have to perform in front of him, makes me feel queasy, frozen. I'm certain I'll fall flat on my face, ruin everything even as the first person steps out. Aleah. And she's still holding my hand.

The stunning blonde is across from me. I turn my back on her only to have Miller in my direct vision. Ian stands behind him, smiling, urging me on.

Aleah doesn't give me time to think, dives into a scene.

She's so expressive, her face so full of emotion, I forget everything around me and react. Fly free of myself and give her everything I have.

I'm aware when she trades out, feel the shift when a handsome guy takes her place. He's more dominant than Aleah, I feel his need to control the scene and ebb around him, allowing him to do so while I support him. And then he's gone and another young woman is there, perky and hilarious. Everything twists into funny and I'm happy to oblige her.

I feel like I've been there, switching personas, forever, when the gorgeous blonde appears before me. I can feel her aggression, but she doesn't engage despite the fact I'm ready to continue. Turns away from me and points at Miller.

"I think she's had enough," she says. "Who's up?"

It's shocking to step back, to glance at my watch and see I've been in the circle for almost a half hour. Aleah scowls at the blonde, Miller, too. He doesn't step out, one of my former partners going instead. I watch and absorb the blonde's performance. She's talented, really talented, and I wish I had the courage to enter the circle again, to challenge her and see what the two of us could do together.

Too late, she turns and leaves our circle. Miller finally takes the center and, on impulse, I join him.

His face crumples, hands lifting to me, shaking as tears moisten his eyes. "I loved you," he says. "And you broke my heart."

I feel his hurt like a living thing, reach for him on impulse. Step away. I'm not acting. I'm living it. And even as I do, I know this, this is where I'm supposed to be. Not just out of myself, but coming back in as a new me. Present as the girl who broke his heart.

"I had to go." Quiet, murmured, my body trembling. "I didn't want you to watch me die."

His eyes widen, hands falling slowly. "But you're alive, here, with me."

"For now," I say. "For a little while."

Miller closes the distance between us, hand

cupping the back of my head, fingers wound in my hair, his other pressed to the small of my back. His lips hover over mine as I feel myself go limp in his arms, breathing in small, sad pants.

"For as long as we have," he whispers. Then kisses me.

I die in his arms.

Applause breaks us apart, Aleah wiping her eyes between claps. I stand, breathless as Miller bows to me.

I shiver at Ian's sad smile before he fades away.

"Like mother, like daughter," he says before backing away to the edge of the circle.

I retreat, too, taking deep breaths, knowing I've finally found exactly what I was looking for. *This was what Mom talked about. Being someone else inside yourself.* I'd been close before, but with Miller, I found it.

And I love it.

I almost cry when the two hours is over and it's time to go. Roger's, "And that's class," breaks my attention and the spell this whole experience has held over me. I spin in a circle, hugging myself, wanting to laugh and weep and squeeze every one of the other actors. I do hug most of them, at least the ones in my circle, thank them for a wicked time. They all seem happy, bouncy and excited, raving about my performances, how much fun they had with me. Their comments are all the same, run together into one big bundle of glowing joy.

I look for Aleah to hug her, too, and see her once again in conversation with the beautiful blonde. But this time they both look angry. Whatever their argument is about, the blonde leaves in a huff, Aleah scowling after her.

And then Miller is beside me, his familiar smile as good as a hug. "You said you were coming with us this time?"

I nod, my nerves jangling, but not wanting this night to ever end. I think of Ian, grateful he hasn't appeared again to shatter my wonderful good humor, and promise myself Miller is just a friend. For now. Maybe, at some point, I'll be willing for it to go further. But I tuck Ian into my heart even as I smile back at Miller.

"Wouldn't miss it," I say.

I'm partway down the stairs when I realize I've forgotten my purse. "Damn," I say to Piper as Miller and Aleah talk, walking down ahead of us, heads close together. "I'll be right with you."

Piper waves, Ruben too, and thud down the stairs, voices loud. I spin back, squeeze with a smile of apology between two people and hurry down the hall back to the room.

It's mostly dark, only a single exit light casting illumination. I spot my purse on a chair by the far wall and go to retrieve it, shaking my head at my own silliness.

Bend to pick it up, mind racing over tonight, the most amazing night I've ever had.

And scream as someone grabs me from behind.

# Chapter Eight

I turn on instinct, nail my attacker with my elbow just like I learned in self-defense class. I hear a grunt, catch a whiff of alcohol and stale weed mixed with pungent aftershave.

Spin to see Roger bent over his ribs, one arm protecting them while he scowls at me.

I let out a shaky breath, sag as I nab my purse and drape it over my shoulder.

"I'm sorry," I say. "But you scared the crap out of me."

He straightens, tossing back his long hair now free of its ponytail. "Nice hit." He winces. Smiles like a leading man on a soap opera. "You impress me more and more, new girl."

"Riley," I say, feeling my tension return as he plants himself in front of me. Between me and the door. "My name is Riley." What is he doing? He can't mean to block my way out. He's just being friendly.

*Riley,* Ian's voice says, the loudest I've heard it in a long time. *Get out. Now.*

"Your scene with Mr. Hill was quiet impressive." Roger doesn't seem to take the hint I'm not interested, leaning closer. From the faint tracing of veins in his eyes, he's had more to drink and probably to smoke than is good for him. "I know a few directors who would love to talk to you, no matter how raw your talent."

That makes me pause. Is he being genuine? Ian scowls over Roger's shoulder, angry, protective. I know better. "Thanks," I say, softening a little despite my growing unease. I can handle this if all he wants is to hit on me a little. Especially if he means it. "That would be great."

Roger's smile turns wolfish. "A little private work with me," one of his hands lifts to land on my waist while Ian's voice shouts at me to run. Roger shuffles closer, head bowing over me, "Some private sessions, and you'll be ready for Broadway."

So, not genuine at all. I need to learn to trust Ian—to trust my instincts feeding Ian's furious apparition. My original assessment Roger just wants to screw me seems to be accurate. Time to go.

I push against him, trying for as nice a rejection as I can come up with, but he just advances on me, forcing me back faster than I'm prepared for. I retreat, knowing I should just hit him and run, but I'm already moving, two chairs squealing over the floor as he forces me between them and toward the wall. My back hits the plaster with a dull thud. Before I can gather my thoughts and my breath, Roger presses close to me, trapping me between the cold brick and his body.

Ian glares at him, unable to help me, as unable as I am to help myself in that terrible moment.

I'm smothering in Roger's rancid scent, the heat of his body, his hands suddenly everywhere as I feel panic for the second time in only a few minutes. But this time I freeze, forgetting my self-defense training in the face of a real assault. I know I should move, act. Instantly blame myself for not just fucking doing something.

*Riley.* Ian's voice is loud in my head.

Heart pounding, lips parted, gasping for air, my body flinches from Roger's roaming touch, my muscles seizing, breath stopping at last as his mouth descends.

And his hand squeezes my breast.

*RILEY!*

Light bursts behind my eyes, smashes my inability to move into a million pieces as Ian's shout shatters my freeze. Reflex lifts my right knee and nails Roger between the legs with all the strength I have.

Roger screams, falls back from me and I can suddenly breathe again, cold air washing over me, his scent still lingering, clinging as I lurch forward, stumbling over him where he writhes on the floor. I stagger past Ian's shade. To the door and out.

Out into the hall stinking of urine and vomit, wanting to add my own puke to it, breath whistling out of my lungs as I pound down the stairs, fly toward the door.

Through it while Ian chases me.

And into Miller's arms.

He holds me as I sob once, clinging to him, shaking. His hand makes soft circles on my back until I pull away, fury finally rising in place of my terror, a surging response to my own weakness.

"Son of a bitch!" I'm snarling like an animal, arms thrashing. I turn and kick the door with the toe of my boot. The glass cracks at the bottom, spiderwebbing out from the point of impact. I've just vandalized the wretched place, but I don't care.

I don't care.

Miller's scowl is so deep he looks like an angel ready to throw off his halo and descend to hell.

"What happened?"

I tell him, voice still shaking, only then realizing the image of Ian is gone and there is only Miller with me. Have to hold him with the full weight of my body to keep him from going back upstairs.

Miller quivers against me, stronger than me by far, but allowing me to keep him here for whatever reason.

"I handled it," I say, fighting to pull myself together, to shake off the irrational rage mixed with loathing I have for my own inability to defend myself, no matter I finally managed to strike back. "He won't be walking for a while." I hope I hurt him so badly he'll never walk again.

Or touch another girl. Like he touched me. My body shudders and I just want to go home and take a shower. Burn my clothes, because that's a rational reaction to being pawed by a disgusting old man.

Miller nods, sharp and tight, though he still strains against me. "I'll make sure everyone knows," he says. "Roger's done."

"I should call the cops." I really, really should. I can't be the only girl he's done this to. But I don't reach for my phone, and Miller's anger turns to sadness.

This isn't a TV show. It's reality. I could report him, try to charge him. Because I don't want this to happen to anyone else. But it's my word against his. For all I know, he might turn this around on me and charge me with assault.

I have no proof. We were alone. Ian's ghost doesn't count.

Pisses me off, knowing Roger will get away with it. Until I absorb the grim look on Miller's face. This is a big city, but a small community. I have a feeling Miller will be good to his word and Roger won't be teaching again, at least not here.

I hate to let it go, but I have no choice.

Miller offers his hand. "I'm sorry. I didn't realize you went back in there alone." I take his fingers in mine, welcome the firm warmth of his skin. "And I had no idea he'd go so far. To my knowledge, he's only ever been a creep in the past."

I suppose I should be flattered. By now, with Miller beside me, the fresh air in my lungs, I've shaken off most of my fear, anger starting to cool. "Not your fault," I say. "Maybe he learned a lesson." The good girl in me whispers maybe I misjudged, overreacted. Asked for it.

No way. I can still feel his hands on me.

I just hope this isn't the norm, or I'll be on my way back home. Already making a plan to protect myself in case there's a next time with someone else, I allow Miller to lead me down the steps, knowing I won't be back here, to this class, regardless.

"I hope this won't make you think about quitting," he says, real concern in his voice, clearly reading my mind.

But no. I'm not going to let one disgusting bastard ruin this when I'm just getting started. I clench my jaw against the already fading memory of Roger's stench and answer. "Not a chance." I flash Miller a smile, refusing to let Roger and his groping hands dominate my night any further.

Miller seems to relax. "You're a natural," he says. "That scene was amazing."

I know exactly how he feels.

Miller pauses, squeezes my hand before letting me go. "If I'd known how good you are," he says, "I would have told you not to bother with Roger. A few of us go because we like the setup. But you won't learn much from him."

*Except to avoid his groping. Yeah.*

"You really want a place to play?" He seems hesitant, shy almost. I'm amazed he's even asking, and that he seems nervous around me of all people. "Because I know the perfect place for you."

I don't know why I trust him so much. But I do.

"Let's go," I say.

# Chapter Nine

We walk in silence, not awkward at all, a lovely, companionable quiet. Miller leads me deeper into Hell's Kitchen, further from the center of the city and toward the water, until we pause in front of what looks like an abandoned warehouse. The top floor is flooded with light, though, and music pours out of the open windows.

I shiver, wondering what I'm getting myself into even as excitement builds.

"Come on," Miller says, his shyness still in place, sweet smile on his lips. I follow him to a side door, the pale blue paint peeling, rust making hardened trickles from a couple of dents. But the lock looks new and the door itself is fairly substantial. I feel eyes on us, know this can't be a great part of the neighborhood as most of the buildings seem more run down, a few corners dominated by working girls in skimpy clothes with dead eyes staring into the night.

I wonder if I'm doing the right thing.

Miller holds the door for me, pulling it shut behind us, not bothering to lock it, sort of defeating the purpose as far as I'm concerned. A creaking elevator carries us from the brightly lit lobby area, worn but clean, up to the top of the building.

The doors open onto a huge space, giant windows on two walls. The source of the light and music. And it's filled with people my age, all laughing, talking. Acting out scenes, from what I can gather, as Miller continues on toward the back of the big room to what looks like an industrial kitchen. Aleah spins, drink in hand, spots me. Comes running, a huge smile on her face. Her lips are moist on my cheek before she pulls away.

"You're here!" She spins me, and I laugh.

"I said I'd come." I look around, breathless with my growing excitement. "What is this place?"

"Miller's," Piper says, handing me a plastic glass with what smells like beer in it. I smile, don't drink it. I hate beer with a passion. I spot Miller, still on the move, heading past the kitchen to a door. He disappears through it, closing it behind him as I gape around.

"This is his house?" It's massive, and though in a rougher part of the city, I know it has to be pricey. "He's rich?" I don't know why that bothers me. No, not bother, not exactly. Just feels like I've uncovered something private about him I instinctively know makes him uncomfortable.

Ruben rolls his eyes, sighs dramatically. "The Great Miller Hill," he says, "is loaded, sweet cheeks."

"Do you all live here?" I can only imagine how amazing it would be, like camping out with the coolest people I've ever met.

"We might as well," Aleah laughs. "And now, so do you."

I take a minute to sneak away, find a quiet corner and call Aunt Vonda. I already warned her I'd be out late, but I want to check in anyway.

"I'm not your mother, pet," she says over the

sound of her TV. "You have fun. Besides, you're young—and you don't work until lunch." Her laughter makes me giggle.

More beer arrives through the elevator with three new players and six giant pizzas five minutes later. I settle on the arm of the couch with my beer traded for soda and a slice of pepperoni in my hands. Miller reappears, coming to sit next to me, changed from his button up into a t-shirt.

I'm expecting some kind of crazy party, my only real experience with this kind of thing the ones I attended when Ian was healthy enough to go. The old shale pit back home made the perfect weekend party spot, though what anyone saw in drinking until they threw up, staggering around, groping each other and smoking weed until they passed out was beyond me.

I needn't have worried. This particular party is nothing like the small town escapism I am used to. For the next few hours, I sing and laugh and join impromptu scenes, read from pages handed to me, try my voice at harmony on show tunes I only vaguely know the melody and words to and learn some new dance moves I'm sure make me look like a clumsy idiot.

I hardly care. Piper continually cracks me up, his flamboyant nature counterpoint to Miller who pairs with him in the most outrageous scenes. I finally accept a cooler from Aleah who wrinkles her nose at the beer, too, "who likes that crap?" and have the most brilliant night in history.

Roger's little aberration is now only a blip on my radar.

This is what I've been craving, what I hoped to find in New York. This is my dream, being surrounded by those who share my passion. I loved rehearsals at home doing theater, the fact the cast felt like family right from day one. But the feeling always faded when the show was over.

This, these people, give me the feeling I'll never lose my family connection again.

I'm shocked and flustered when Miller pulls Piper to a halt after a particular scene and raises his glass to me.

"Roger Doger," he says while the others groan, "decided our darling Riley," all eyes turn to me and now my cheeks are on fire, "was a blow up doll earlier." I freeze for the second time that night, feeling like I'm being assaulted all over again as he goes on. "What do we do to those who think groping actors is allowed?"

A moment of utter silence falls when my bubble bursts, and I am suddenly afraid they'll hate me for what happened, blame me somehow.

And then, in a roar, they boo and hiss and curse. At Roger.

"The ass," Piper says, rushing over, hugging me. "He'll never teach again."

They all nod, offer me condolences and suggestions for punishment while I gape and feel tears threaten at their support.

From that moment, if I hadn't felt loved already, they surround me, engage me in every activity, fighting over me at times while I laugh and do my best to make everyone happy. Miller's beaming face flashes in my view from time to time, Aleah glued to one hip, Piper to the other.

"Silly," Aleah whispers in my ear at one point. "I saw the fear on your face. But shit like that? Don't fly, not with us. We look out for each other. Because no one else is going to."

Very good to know.

I'm belting out the alto part of "Seasons Of Love", the theme song from *Rent*, when my eyes drift to the window. And the sight of the sky turning pale orange. It's morning already? I don't want the night to end, feel more energized and full of power than I ever have.

This has been the most incredible night of my life.

Aleah and Piper suddenly fade, as though morning casts some spell over them. They cuddle together, Ruben with his head on Piper's lap, on the end of the couch as I sink to the arm and look around. Realize, with a blush of modesty, some of my new friends have paired off, are murmuring to each other in dark corners in the most intimate ways.

I think it's time to go. Stand and see Miller watching me. He rises from his chair, comes to my side, leads me toward the elevator as though knowing what I'm thinking.

"I want to show you something," he says.

We go up instead of down, rising to the roof. I step out into the early light of morning and breathe deep, catching the hint of salt from the Hudson, the flashes of sun passing across windows of the distant high rises. Miller and I stand on the edge of the roof, leaning over the wall, looking at New York, so beautiful in the dawn.

"Thank you," I say, wishing I had better words. "Tonight was a dream." A dream come true, not just fantasy.

He meets my eyes, his almost transparent in the sunlight. "You belong with us," he says.

I want to agree, hope he's right. The last few hours are everything I've ever imagined my life could be. "Is it like this every night?"

He laughs, pushes back his golden hair. "Most nights," he says.

"It's generous of you," I say, suddenly remembering he's rich and maybe I should act differently around him. But no, he's Miller to me. Whatever his financial status.

Miller shrugs. "I like having people around," he says, voice darkening, frowning at the city a moment before his mood lightens again. "I hope you'll be back."

It's odd, I feel like I've learned more tonight than I did in both classes with Roger. "I will," I say. "Maybe you could recommend a good school, too." I've made up my mind I'm going for it. "I want to act for a living."

So amazing to say it out loud. Miller grins.

"As if there was any doubt of that," he says, leaning toward me to tap the end of my nose with his index finger. He's very close to me, close enough I can see the sparkle deep in his gaze, the soft stubble on his chin. The laugh lines around his eyes and mouth.

The morning breathes in, the sound of the city soft in the background as Miller leans closer. His breath is warm on my skin, the tip of his nose brushing over mine as his mouth descends. My lips part, eyes drifting closed.

And the image of Ian appears out of nowhere. Reminding me of everything I'm about to throw away with this one kiss.

I pull away from Miller with a soft meep of surprise before I can stop myself, guilt hitting me in the chest with the blow of a hammer. Miller's own shock is edged by concern.

"Riley, I'm sorry." He steps back. "I'm such an insensitive ass. After what you went through tonight—"

I shake my head, hands now trembling, knees weakened, willing Ian away so hard the phantom vanishes. Leaving more guilt behind. "No, it's okay," I flap my hands at him like that will clear the air. Tension has returned, tightens my shoulders, making it hard to breathe. "I have to go."

I turn and run away from him, wishing I wasn't such a coward, that, for once, Ian would leave me alone. Then guilt, around and around in a circle of punishment, even as Miller calls my name.

The elevator doors close on him before he can reach me and I'm sobbing into the small space, hating how I just ruined the best night of my life.

# Chapter Ten

I pull myself together as I hurry for home, head down, ignoring the early morning traffic, catcalls from a construction crew who take a moment to make me feel like meat. *So nice of them to be such assholes when I already hate myself.*

Aunt Vonda is gathering her purse at the door when I walk into the apartment, gives a quick cry of joy before hugging me.

"I'm sorry I'm so late," I say. "I didn't mean to worry you."

She leans away, shaking her head. "I wasn't," she says. "Maybe I should have been. But you sounded so happy on the phone."

I'm frankly shocked. I expected a lecture. She must see so in my face because she wrinkles her nose.

"You're a grown woman," she says, patting my hand, hefting her giant bag over one arm. "And I'm not my brother."

Dad would have thrown a fit. Told me this was the kind of behavior he warned me about. Partying all night, though it's not like me at all.

Pisses me off he ended up being right.

"I'm usually more responsible." Why do I feel the need to explain myself to her? Because it's true?

"Riley Ellen James." Aunt Vonda sets her bag down, grasps both of my hands in hers. "You have been nothing but a pet and a dear since you arrived. It's been a pleasure having you. You had the courtesy to call. And it's not as though I didn't expect something like this to happen."

I stare at her, mute. She expected me to be out all night?

"Your mother and I were friends, remember?" Aunt Vonda lets me go, retrieves her bag. "I even went to a party or two with her." She laughs, rolls her eyes, pats at her hair like someone's admiring her. "The most fun I've ever had."

The tight ball in the pit of my stomach loosens as I finally let go of the guilt over Miller and Ian. And remember the party.

Grin before I can stop myself. "The most fun ever," I say.

"It's not your fault." She looks distressed a moment. "Your mother. Your father. Marie was Rick's whole world. Losing Marie so young, and with you looking just like her…"

She doesn't have to apologize for Dad. "I know," I say. Wishing I could forgive him for being an asshole all these years, but not quite getting there.

Aunt Vonda laughs. "I can tell you're not drunk," she says. Sniffs. "And you don't smell like marijuana." She shrugs. "And you're home safe and sound." She kisses my cheek, squeezing past me. "As long as you're not late for work," she shakes a finger at me, grinning, "I have no complaints."

"I won't be." I wave at her as she leaves, hugging myself in the sudden quiet of the apartment, only the hum of her refrigerator and the air conditioning breaking the silence.

I go to my room, brush my teeth. Stare at myself in the mirror for a minute, looking at my pale auburn hair, my light green eyes. The dusting of the faintest freckles on my nose and cheeks. Mom's face.

I miss her so much right now. She would have loved the party, too. I just know it. I retreat to bed, lie down, try to sleep. But I just can't, not with the night playing over in my mind, making me giggle, sigh and obsess over every detail.

Returning always to that final moment when Miller tried to kiss me.

I roll over and stare at the picture by my bed. The one of Ian and me, back when he was still okay on the outside, if not the inside. Still had his head of dark hair, the glow in his hazel eyes. And then I'm crying and trying not to, wiping at the tears as fast as they come.

There was a time my mind would have conjured him, imagine him tucked against my back, spooning me, murmuring in my ear. When I could almost feel his arm around my waist, the heat of his thin body pressed to mine.

But not now, with the morning sun peeking in my window, no matter how hard I try to call him to me. Staring at his picture does me no good, and though I consider getting up, turning on my laptop, watching a video of him just in case such an act would make a difference, I don't.

Things are different, now. Ian stays away. This time, while I'm looking at him, Miller's face is the one that appears, the touch of his skin on mine, the heat of his breath. Blocking out the memory of my love.

I'm not ready to let Ian go.

If only I really believed that was the case.

Instead of arguing with myself, I press my face into my pillow and do my best to send Miller away, too.

I hand over a bundle of tulips to a smiling Asian woman and lean against the counter, stifling a yawn behind my hand as the doorbell rings on her way out. A small line of customers waits for me and I force a smile and the appearance of perkiness.

Three cups of strong coffee and I was up and moving after a failed attempt to sleep. Caffeine or not, I'm really starting to feel the thirty-six hours I've been awake. Still, it's easy to keep a smile on my face. Now I've pushed past my Ian moment, I'm buzzing with excitement for tonight even while I argue with myself.

I don't think I'm going to be able to keep up this pace. But I'm happy to try.

As the day goes on, my mind whirling around my departure to the loft and my new friends, I start to wonder. Should I just show up at Miller's? Or maybe I pissed him off, running away like that. Maybe I screwed up whatever it was we might have had. I have myself half-convinced to just get my ass over there with the other side arguing I should let him make another first move when the doorbell rings and I glance past my latest customer.

I see Aleah grinning at me and Piper bouncing off Ruben next to her.

I smile back, all my worries gone as Miller waves, smiles too.

After I finish with the mother and daughter, my friends drift forward to take their place. Piper hops up on the counter, sniffing a carnation he stole from an arrangement as Miller leans over, blue eyes full of amusement.

"Yet again, we see a great actress in her natural

habitat."

I blush, shake my head while Aleah laughs.

"Beats waiting tables, sugar," she says while Ruben's "Amen!" is echoed by Piper.

"Can I help you with some flowers?" He wants to play, I can play. Funny how taking off this morning doesn't seem to matter in the face of his teasing. Nor does the fact Ian doesn't cross my mind except in a fleeting moment of memory.

"Yes, please," Miller says. "Two orders. Another dozen long stems, if you would be so kind."

Aleah makes a face, crosses her arms over her chest. "Like she deserves them," she says. I have no idea who she's talking about, but Piper seems to agree with the sentiment, sighing dramatically as he hops off the counter and bumps hips with Ruben.

The gorgeous Hispanic frowns. "You have no idea," he says. "She's brilliant."

"Right, I forgot." Piper hangs from his boyfriend who shrugs him off. "Forgive me. The Queen Of All Acting is your new bestie."

I wish I knew what they are talking about, but instead focus on what I'm doing, writing down Miller's order despite my burning curiosity. And because my heart is pounding with worry. Who is she and why is he buying her roses?

And why do I care? We're friends...

"And a single daisy," Miller says, startling me. "Please, miss."

Weird. I turn to the glass case as Aleah rests her chin on her hand and watches me.

"You were incredible last night," she says in a wistful tone.

Damn this blushing. I see Aunt Vonda grinning, minding her own business at the back of the work area. Sure she is.

"Thanks," I say. And then gush as I pull roses

from the bucket, the chill of the case giving me goosebumps as much as my memories of last night. "So are you! I've never heard anyone sing like that." Her voice made me cry, the love ballad she sang at the party heartbreakingly beautiful.

"You haven't heard anything," Piper says, pushing his way between Aleah and Miller. "Make sure you give her enough to drink and she'll sing you some gospel." He swoons into Miller who supports him with a grin on his face. "Died and gone to heaven, muffin."

Aleah hums a quick tune and shrugs.

"My daddy may not have left me much," she practically sings the words, "but he did give me his voice."

"Can I get a halleluiah," Piper says.

I carefully wrap the roses as my friends all dutifully chorus back to him, myself included. And, to my giggling surprise, so does Aunt Vonda.

She peeks around the large arrangement she's making, a hopeful look on her face. "Maybe you'll give us a little right now?"

Aleah grins. "For you, anything," she says.

And breaks into "Amazing Grace".

By the time she hits the chorus, I'm crying all over myself. Verse two has me sniffing at the cash register, unable to see the buttons. I have to stop and listen. I'm not here in the shop anymore. I'm with Aleah, my mind on the deck of a rolling ship with seagulls crying overhead as I remember this song is not about religion, but about slavery and one man's choice to beg God for forgiveness. I don't come home to myself, perfectly still until the last line, "was blind, but now I see," breaks over me like a wave. I'm clapping, Aunt Vonda is beside me, clapping, the three new customers waiting behind them are clapping and Aleah takes a bow. Blows Aunt Vonda a kiss.

My aunt clasps her hands to her chest, shivering with barely-held happiness. "Thank you, my dear," she says, as choked up as I am.

Miller hands me his credit card while Aunt Vonda sighs and goes back to her arrangement. I wipe away my tears, Aleah speaking to one of the customers waiting in a low voice.

"Who are the roses for?" I really couldn't be more blatant about it, but Aleah's song has shattered my control.

Miller's eyebrows rise a little. He just takes his card back with a smile. "Actually," he says, "I was going to invite you to come along to deliver them, if you can."

"Where are you going?" And then it hits me. Silly, the flowers are for an actor. Just like the last dozen he ordered.

*I'm such an idiot.*

"There's an opening tonight," he says. "A great show, we all know the lead."

Aleah has just rejoined us, her jaw tightening as he speaks. "We think we do," she says.

Miller glances at her, but doesn't comment. I notice her crossed arms, her tapping fingers on her forearm. "I think you'll like it," he says.

I really want to go. "I work until seven," I say, not wanting to ask Aunt Vonda, suddenly awake again and sure I can go another night without sleep.

"Perfect," Miller says, taking the bundle of roses into his hands, leaving the lone daisy in its tiny sleeve of plastic behind. "The show starts at eight. I'll meet you here at 7:30?"

Aunt Vonda is beside me, almost breathless in her need to speak. "Leave tonight's cleanup for me in the morning," she says. "Have fun!"

I gape at her before turning and nodding at Miller.

"Thanks," I say. "I'd love to."

"A queen," Piper pronounces, bowing with Shakespearian flourish to Aunt Vonda who giggles and blushes. "A queen among a garden of Eden."

Ruben hums a bar of music and the pair sings the line in perfect harmony.

Aunt Vonda laughs out loud, shoos them off. Aleah blows me a kiss, Miller turning away with a little wave. I wave back, glance down.

He's forgotten his daisy. I grab it, even as I call his name.

Miller turns back. "It's for you," he says.

I hold the white flower in my shaking hands as the door swings shut behind him and it's not until the sweet lady who's next in line whispers, "Excuse me," that I snap out of it.

*He gave me a daisy. Ian's flower.* I'm not sure if it's a bad thing, or only makes things more complicated.

The craziest part is how did Miller know?

# Chapter Eleven

I stand outside the storefront of Aunt Vonda's flower shop, bouncing in my toes, my sandals a little too tall for the motion, making me wobbly. I managed to run home for five minutes on my break—at Aunt Vonda's insistence—and pull a dress out of my closet, a pair of heels. I didn't have time to do much with my hair, but a bit of mascara and lipstick and I'm good to go.

I even raced through the cleanup of the shop at the end of my shift, not wanting to leave it for Aunt Vonda. She's been so amazing to me, she doesn't deserve to come in to a mess in the morning.

A miracle, I'm even five minutes early, nervously pacing in front of the windows, using one to check my teeth for lipstick when I spot Miller crossing the street, his reflection approaching me through the glass.

I spin to face him, tottering on my feet, cursing the stupid shoes and my choice even as he comes to my side and smiles.

Everything fades when Miller smiles.

"You look beautiful." He kisses my cheek, a soft and familiar gesture as though I've known him forever. I lean into him when he does.

He's stunning, as usual, though it's the first time I've seen him in a suit.

"You too," I say, hating how I can't come up with something better.

Miller doesn't seem to mind, leading me down the street, back the way he came. "The show is Off-Broadway," he says. "Have you been to many yet?"

I shake my head, hanging on to his arm, partially for balance, partially because I like the way he feels next to me. "None," I say, realizing how silly that is. "I need to start."

He nods. "Part of the job," he says. "You'll hate me for it, though." His burst of deep laughter warms me past the mild evening. I catch a glimpse of Ian's sad face in a shop window as we walk by, flinch from the image though the memory of my dead boyfriend keeps his distance. "You'll never attend a play or film for fun again. It's too great an opportunity to learn."

I choose to focus on Miller. And despite his need to warn me about dissecting story, I truly love that part. "I know what you mean," I say, feeling shy about talking with him, knowing he has far more experience than I do. "I love watching for that reason."

He guides me through a cross walk toward a glowing marquis, "The Favored" written in plastic letters across the top, "Starring Bianca Sullivan" underneath. "That's what I love about you," he says. "You're already thinking like a pro."

I'm blushing, wish I could turn off my thrill like a faucet. Did he say he loves me...? *Don't say anything.* I precede him inside when he holds the door for me, knowing it was just a figure of speech, wondering why I suddenly hope it's really more.

Ian waves gently from the glass and fades away, leaving me to ponder this sudden switch in longing for him to Miller.

The air is cool, a subtle tap on the cheek from the crispness of it pulling me back to reality the rest of the way. I swallow my guilt to the sound of the soft murmur of people, muted in the small lobby. Miller hands me a ticket, the edges rimmed in red, a small logo marking the top and I reach for my purse, my wallet. But he shakes his head.

"Comps," he says. "Freebies. On me." Laughs.

"So gallant," I say. "That's okay, I'm a cheap date." And hope he doesn't see me gasp for air.

This isn't a date.

Miller laughs again. "Good to know," he says. "I'm not."

We enter, a young woman in a black vest and red bowtie handing us programs. Miller waves her off when she offers to show us our seats while I step inside the theater and look up at the lights. The red curtain. The stage.

And my heart swells with joy. Magical, mystical, a place of dreams and make believe more real than the world outside. At least, to me. I'm suddenly a little girl again, Mom holding my hand, standing by a stage as she talks with other people who radiate the kind of charisma she does. And then I'm at school, face thick with makeup, dressed in a gown made by one of my classmates. To the small theater at home, the heat of the lights, the hum of the waiting audience.

This. Whether on the stage side of the curtain or here in the seats, this is where I belong.

Miller's hand on my elbow breaks the spell, but only partially, enough to let him inside the coiling magic. I allow the dim sounds to take over, the scent of perfumes mingling with the heat of the bright bulbs overhead, absorbed by plush red chairs. Orderly rows, the seat cushions tucked up out of the way, marked with numbers and letters, leading in curved grace from the center aisle. The theater is already filling, forcing me to move forward as they gather behind me at the top of the aisle.

Miller guides me down the sloping stairs close to the front while I look around like a child in a toy store. I spot Aleah as she turns to look, almost leaves her seat in her enthusiasm to wave at us. Piper and Ruben sit beside her, slapping at each other and laughing in some silly game.

Aleah comes to the end of the aisle and hugs me, pulling me down beside her while Miller takes the outside seat. The bundle of roses rolls as my sandal hits them, but Miller rescues them before they can drop down under the row in front of me.

Aleah hooks her arm through mine. "I'm so happy you're here, Riley Skyley."

I can only grin at her, a kid having her best Christmas of all time.

"I don't come to Bianca's shows anymore," Aleah says. "But she's a friend of Miller's, so…"

I look at him with curiosity. He shrugs, face darkening. "Not really," he says. "But I like to support other actors."

His thigh brushes against mine, though I doubt he notices. I'm acutely aware of his proximity, how easy it would be to drop my head on his shoulder, for his arm to go around mine. I catch a flicker of motion on the stage, look up.

Ian is watching. Face blank, quiet. But it's not the kind, sweet Ian I like to remember. This make-believe ghost is Ian at his worst. Thin, ragged, face shrunken, body wasted to the edge of life. The Ian I did my best to forget.

Why my imagination is conjuring him now, this way… I turn my head, close my eyes. Open them again as the lights flicker.

Miller meets my gaze, his steady, thoughtful.

"Five minutes," he says.

Impulse drives me to speak. "Have you ever wondered, if things happened differently, where you'd be? What you'd be doing?" Ian's image won't leave me alone, following my gaze, standing beside Miller at the end of the aisle. All I can see of him in my mind's eye is his thin hand, an IV dangling, the baggy pajama bottoms he died in.

Miller leans closer, eyes locked on mine. "I wonder that all the time," he says. "But we can't go back, Riley. All we can do is the best with what we have, right now." He pauses. "Regrets?"

I shake my head, eyes stinging as Ian's image finally fades and leaves me be. "No," I say. "Just... sometimes I wonder, that's all."

Miller squeezes my hand.

Did I just lie to him? I turn my head, look up at the empty stage. I think of Ian and how he's been such a huge part of my life. Clearly he still is, though I'm beginning to wish I hadn't spent the last year ingraining into myself this need to see him everywhere. Do I regret any of it?

No, not regret. But... for the first time, sitting here with Miller, with my new life spreading out in front of me, lit by the stage lights and fed by the murmurs of excitement and anticipation of the waiting audience, I think maybe it's time to let Ian go.

That I'm ready after all.

The lights suddenly go out and I allow myself to just relax and enjoy the show. To not think about Ian or my guilty pleasure of keeping him with me or the fact Miller's leg presses into mine.

When the curtain goes up, I forget.

I forget everything.

The beautiful blonde from class crosses the stage and begins her opening line and I'm instantly captivated. Yes, she was rude to me once, but that is nothing compared to her acting.

I hold my breath as she performs for the next two and a half hours, on the edge of my seat at times. She is brilliant and incredible and I'm in complete idolization mode by the time intermission rolls around.

Miller leaves a few moments, returns with a bottle of water. I can barely speak, smiling at him in what I'm sure is a dazed way. Sit back and allow the others to talk around me, absorbing what I just witnessed. And when the curtain rises again, I'm ready, willing, open to the second act.

Bianca draws me in completely. There might as well not be anyone else on stage. Everything about her performance tells me she gets it, Mom's secret. And I can't wait to actually meet her, introduce myself and talk to her about it.

I'm on my feet when the curtain falls for the closing of the second act, clapping so hard my hands ache. The entire audience rises, a standing ovation for a wonderful performance. I'm grinning, cheeks on fire, but unable to stop as the cast emerges one at a time and takes their bows. I'm sure I'm part of the reason they do three curtain calls before the lights to the theater finally come up and I'm left, breathless and clutching my hands to my chest, so wound up I don't think I'll ever sleep again.

Miller's smile makes it all the more incredible. He bends and retrieves the flowers before stepping into the emptying aisle and gesturing for me to walk ahead of him.

"Shall we meet the star?" His blue eyes sparkle in the lights.

I can't wait.

# Chapter Twelve

I follow Miller to the lobby, gently slipping through the crowd gathered in the small space, chatting about the show. My hand is slippery and damp on the crumpled program I hold, and I have to shake out my fingers to keep them from cramping. I still feel the sting of my palms from all the clapping I did, but it's worth it. So worth it when Miller guides me, with his fingers wound through my opposite ones, to a side door, painted dull black and barely noticeable. He doesn't even look at the guy with a nametag who waves us on. I glance back over my shoulder, cheeks aching from my excited smile, and see Aleah has hooked arms with Piper on one side and Ruben on the other. The three of them sing a tune I don't know, their voices suddenly loud as we pass through the door, and I wonder if they are making it up as they go along.

I'm too wrapped up in the moment to pay close enough attention to find out. As soon as we step into the dark hallway on the other side, I'm in heaven. Backstage bustles with people, most in black clothing, the crew rushing about to complete their after-show tasks. I dodge a young man carrying an extension cord as thick as my wrist, losing my grip on Miller as I do. I reach for him again at the exact moment he reaches back for me.

He laughs over his shoulder.

I look around as if I've never been backstage at a show before, because this one is nothing like the shows I've been part of. Yes, the activity is similar, the people, but these are all pros. The energy feels professional, not the giddy horsing around I'm used to.

Miller heads for the dressing room at the far end of the narrow hall. I glance to my left, see through the wings and out onto the stage, the curtain now up as the crew resets for tomorrow night's show. It's a beautiful view from here, alluring, calling to me to step out past the hoisted curtain and onto the stage, even in the empty house, and say something.

Anything.

And then we're past, slipping by a pair of actors chattering their way out, still in their stage makeup, smelling of sweat and peppermint, until the last door in the hall looms. There's a star on it, a sliver of gold paint left behind as though it had been lovingly applied there ages ago but was left to fade. Not that it matters, because I know what it means and who is behind it.

I'm suddenly nervous and fangirling. I can't wait to finally be introduced to Bianca officially, to talk to her about her performance, to ask her if she knows how crazy talented she is.

Miller reaches for the door handle just as it jerks open. My new idol stands on the other side, blonde hair down from the updo she wore in the last act, dressed in a thin robe hanging open to show her lace bra, her skin still heavy with makeup.

"Bianca." Miller leans in, kisses her cheek as she turns her face to him. Her eyes rove over the rest of us, settle on me. I feel my mouth open, about to blurt my adoration, when Miller hands her the flowers. Her eyes fall to them, to his hand holding mine just as he releases me. I miss the warmth of his touch and look up to see Bianca accepting the bouquet I carefully created to celebrate tonight.

She's frowning as she lets them dangle from her hand like a burden, the plastic wrap unopened and I feel a tiny hurt she doesn't appreciate them. *Silly, she has no idea who wrapped them or, even more, couldn't care less I put them together for her.* I feel more for Miller who seems crestfallen she ignores them so easily.

Aleah snaps her fingers, coming to my side. "You going to let us in?"

Bianca's eyes narrow, but she stands aside without a word. Miller moves past her with a murmur that sounds like an apology for Aleah as my glamorous friend sweeps by like a dusky queen examining her realm for the first time. Piper pauses, arm around his boyfriend, so Ruben can kiss Bianca's cheek, though I notice Piper doesn't follow suit. I see her eyes roll before she turns away. Watch her dump the carefully wrapped roses on the chair next to her makeup table and turn, arms crossing over her chest.

I'm making excuses for her lack of welcome. She must be tired, probably just wants to have a shower and get out of here. But I hear someone pause behind me, her name spoken and, in that instant, I see Bianca light up as though none of us are in the room.

When her admirer continues on without entering, Bianca's dull, irritated expression returns and my heart staggers. Still, I shouldn't judge her. She's brilliant.

I open my mouth to tell her everything—how much I admire her, want to talk to her about the craft.

Miller speaks up first. "Bianca Sullivan," he says, "this is Riley James."

She raises one eyebrow at me. Gives me the once over as though we've never met, as though she didn't kick me out of the improv circle the other night. And says, "So I hear you think you can act."

My whole world begins to crumble the moment I realize she isn't who I saw on stage, not the person I hoped I could connect with, talk with. It all falls apart completely when she crushes my last hope she might actually like me, maybe. All my excitement, the thrill of what I just witnessed, shatters as my open heart closes over like a dying flower too long in the sun without water.

Aleah turns on her with an instant scowl, Miller lurching forward with a muttered, "Bianca," in a disapproving tone. But I'm still staring at the beautiful blonde who ruined the moment out of spite or whatever reason she's chosen to be a bitch. And my admiration burns into ashes.

"I just wanted to tell you how brilliant you were," I say, voice hollow, dim in my ears. I'm amazed I'm able to speak at all. Turn on my heel and leave, feeling numb and broken, wanting nothing more than to escape backstage. Ian appears to me, his dying form making things that much worse. It's suddenly claustrophobic for me, now. As though everyone is staring as Ian's dying face is staring, like I don't belong there. And I don't, I really don't.

I just have to get out to the street and breathe.

Hands grasp me, turn me around in the path of one of the crew who snaps at me, "Be careful." Miller pulls me aside, but I'm dragging him, this time, toward the door. Out into the lobby. Past the glass doors and into the open air.

"Riley, I'm sorry." Miller tugs me to a halt, hugs

me suddenly, breath tickling my ear as my numbness fades at last. Leaving a nasty hurt behind, a little girl's hurt that she doesn't understand or deserve. "Bianca can be such a bitch sometimes."

I shrug it off, shrug him off, backing away, the heel of my sandal catching a crack in the sidewalk. He grabs me before I can fall, holds me upright as I steady my breathing.

"It's fine," I say. While dying Ian weeps over Miller's shoulder, fueling my pain and loss. And his. His imagined empathy, that of the instant destruction of my hope, my moment of need to connect with someone through my mother's talent and memory.

"It's not." He lets me go. "She's just jealous. I should have known."

Jealous? I shake my head, sniff so my nose won't run, so I won't sob like a baby. "Of what?"

Miller laughs softly. "She's seen you act," he says.

So? "I don't understand." His words mean nothing to me, not while Ian cries and his face crumples in sadness and illness, telling me to run, get away, be safe from hurt. To escape back into my fantasies and forget any of this happened.

"Riley," Miller says, stepping closer, blocking my imaginary commune with my dead boyfriend, breaking the hold the hurt has over me. His hand settles gently on my elbow, eyes earnest. "She's jealous of you."

I laugh in his face, practically choke on it. "You're cracked." Bianca has nothing to be jealous of.

Miller's smile is sweet, kind. "You have no idea," he says. And turns away. Spins back. I can see the shift in him, he's not himself anymore and I feel, despite the lingering pain, a thrill all the way to my toes even as I look around, self-conscious.

*What is he doing? Acting? Right here on the street?*

"You left me too soon, Delores," he says. I know that name. It's one of the scenes we played at the night before. And I know what comes next. But I'm flustered, aware of the people still emerging from the theater, watching now. Wondering what he's up to as Miller falls to one knee. "You left me a broken man."

I can't do this, just act. On cue. And yet, I can, I have. That's what acting is all about. Still, this is different, surrounded by strangers, people who have just come from seeing Bianca perform.

She's a pro and I'm just...

Just what? I look up, expecting Ian to be there, still sad.

He's gone. And so is my moment of loss in the face of what I love.

My body takes over. I lean away from Miller, eyes downcast. And I pour myself into the part even as the outside world fades away.

And comes back, crisp and clear and full of hurt as Delores tells Horatio why she left him.

The scene is painful and raw. Lost children, death and betrayal. I'm aching inside, Delores devouring me with her grief and need to strike out at her husband. And Miller takes it, feeds it back to me as Horatio.

I love every second of it.

When the scene ends, Miller holding me close, I break from the moment to the sound of applause. For me and for him. And I laugh. He lets me go with a kiss to my cheek, grips my hand. Turns me to face the circle of theater patrons and passers-by who smile and clap and throw money on the ground at our feet.

As though I'm worthy.

# Chapter Thirteen

We bow, together, once, twice. The third time I'm laughing and out of breath, waving like a queen, feeling the best I have since last night. Better even.

This is the culmination of my dream, my desire, my need. Not only to act. But to act for others.

Maybe it's wrong to want their praise. But why act if not for the enjoyment of an audience?

The crowd thins, ends their applause as Aleah and Piper rush to us, hugging us, Ruben hanging back. It's not until I see him standing next to Bianca I realize she's witnessed at least part of what we just did.

And I can't help but smile at her.

"That," Aleah gushes all over me, "was amazing, my sister." She kisses me on the mouth before doing the same to Miller. "You two are stunning together."

Miller bows to her while Piper gathers up our busking proceeds, "They'll be here all week," he tells the fading crowd, and hands the cash to me with a pert grin.

I lose sight of Bianca, not caring now, heart healed as Miller helps me stuff the money into my purse, refusing to accept a single bill. "You earned it," he whispers in my ear. "Bravo, Riley."

The power of the performance has swept Bianca's nasty attack away, left me feeling giddy and bouncy. I know I'm exhausted. I need sleep more than anything, but I'm already being led down the street while Aleah sings us on, Piper in counterpoint though Ruben is missing, back toward Miller's loft.

I'm not sure how much longer I can take the ups and downs of this life. But I'm willing to find out, now more than ever.

I crash on the couch, heels set aside, letting my body rest while the party begins without me. It takes energy to call Aunt Vonda who laughs on the other end.

"You sound like you're falling asleep," she says. "Have fun."

I snort, but she's already hanging up. I tuck my phone into my purse, smiling. I do need to have fun. But when I stand to go to the kitchen, to try to find some coffee to keep me going, I hear Miller say my name.

Turn to find everyone holding up their glass to me.

"To Riley," he says. "For the most amazing street performance I've ever been part of."

Everyone cheers and I realize they were all there, at the show, in the audience. I'm blushing and curtsying, hurrying to the kitchen to avoid their whistles and calls for me to come back and do it again.

I lean against the counter, facing the sink, unable to wipe the smile from my face. When I feel someone beside me, I look up, expecting Aleah, or Miller.

It's Bianca. I had no idea she was here. I open my mouth to again try to tell her she was fantastic, feeling guilty Miller toasted me when she's clearly the star tonight.

Only to have her shoot me down one more time.

"You think you're hot shit," she snarls, low and poisonous, only for my ears. "But you can't handle the pressure, small town." Her scent washes over me, fresh flowers mingling with something like honey. She rolls her eyes, expressive mouth twisting in an ugly scowl, blonde hair silken as it brushes over my hand. "I've seen your type come and go, all shiny and expecting the world to hand you something. Let me tell you, this town will crush you like the pathetic little worm you are."

I'm gaping at her, floored by her vitriol. Unable to react. Any need I felt to share with her the secret, the fact I know why she's so good or to talk about my mother, is gone with her words.

"The first critic who tears you to shreds will kill you," she says. "I can see it in your eyes. You're too weak to handle it. You think that little street scene makes you special?" She snorts, delicate, but carrying volumes. "That having Miller Hill like you means you're a star?" She snaps her fingers in front of my face. "Try a stage show, princess. Try eight shows a week when you have a cold or the flu or can't walk straight because you've been on your feet for so long. Try the long slog and then come back and prove you're an actor."

My mouth opens and closes, but nothing comes out. I want to tell her I can handle it, that she's wrong. I love it too much to go back now.

Bianca's not done. She leans even closer, her lip gloss catching my hair as her mouth brushes my ear. "Trust me, pumpkin," she says with false charm, "just quit while you're ahead."

"Bianca." Aleah's voice breaks the moment. The starlet leans away from me, takes a casual sip of her red wine, looks at my friend through heavy lashes, a sultry smile on her face.

"Aleah." She pushes away from the counter, saunters past. "Just offering some advice to small town."

Aleah scowls after her as I turn and watch Bianca sway her way into the crowd. Ruben kisses her cheek as she enters the group and she hugs him, the center of attention while I cringe against the counter and do my best not to throw up.

I need to get out of here, to just leave and go home. Because my fear Bianca is right is more powerful than anything else at this moment. Haven't I just been through a roller coaster of doubt and excitement? The fear I can't take much more of it?

Who am I fooling thinking I can just come to New York and this will all work out?

Aleah must know how I'm feeling. She's on top of me, pressing me back, one hand on my arm before I can take a step.

"You listen to me, now," she says right in my ear, as intimate as Bianca, but with heart and affection and intensity. "And pay attention, because I'm only going to say this once." I choke on a bitter laugh at the Roger reference, an additional reminder it's going to take way more than the excitement of a few nights fooling around, playing at being an actor, to make it a reality. "There are going to be haters, Riley. People who treat you like crap, who beat you up emotionally because they are afraid."

"Of what?" I meet her eyes, mine burning.

"Of you," she says. "Of failing. Of their own success. There's a shit-load of fear out there, sugar, and none of it," she squeezes my arm, "has anything to do with you. You get me?"

I shake my head. I really don't.

She sighs, breath warm on my cheek. "There will always be critics who hate you because they love to hate. And bitches like Bianca who can't see past their own insecurity." I start at that. Bianca doesn't seem insecure. And she's so talented. "The higher you rise, sweets, the further the fall. Unless."

I wait, quivering under her touch. Wanting to call Ian, his sweet face. For comfort. Just to see him so I don't have to listen to what she's saying.

But I don't and he stays away as my friend goes on.

"You're not alone, baby," Aleah says, so much warmth in her voice I sag under it. "That's the key. Why do you think we're all here together like this?" She waves toward the main room, though her voice doesn't change volume, nor do her eyes leave mine. "We love each other, have fun together. But we're here for support. For those times the haters try to drag us down."

"What happens when one of you is the hater?" I feel my own hate rising, now. Against Bianca for her little speech and her arrogance and a seed of it aimed at myself for being such a weakling.

Aleah shrugs. "It happens," she says, though her eyes tighten around the corners as though she's thinking her own terrible thoughts about Bianca. "Thing is, the haters aren't in it for the rest of us. They're only in it for themselves. That's the difference."

I nod. I can see that. Glance sideways at Bianca who has made herself the center of everything, talking louder than the others, planting herself front and center so they all notice her.

"She craves it," Aleah says. "She needs it to survive. You just love it."

It's true. I'm just as happy to sit outside the excitement and cheer others on. The fear cracks open, the shock of Bianca's sudden attack fading as I feel myself relax.

"I want you to remember one more thing," Aleah

says, drawing my gaze back to her dark eyes. "When the critics are bastards, when the bitches converge. When you feel like quitting. I want you to remember what it felt like on that street." She pokes me gently in the chest. "Tonight. With Miller. Because the fame, the fortune, the hangers on, all of it, Riley Skyley. None of it compares to how what we do *feels*."

She's so right. I'm smiling again, falling into the memory of Delores and Horatio. I shake free Bianca's attempt to chase me off and straighten.

Hug Aleah tight. "Thank you," I say. While a tiny little part of me holds tight to the fear maybe, just maybe, Bianca is right.

"Sister," Aleah whispers, drowning out the morsel of anxiety with her luscious voice, "we've all been there. Me, too." She shrugs as I let her go. "Still happens sometimes. Point is, we keep going. Because we don't just act. We are actors."

I nod. Rub my arm with one hand where goosebumps have risen. Glare at Bianca's back in an attempt to firm up my backbone and use anger to kill the last of my fear.

"Got it," I say. "Except."

Aleah waits.

"If she's right," I say, forcing myself to voice it, to drag it out into the light instead of allowing the idea to fester. "If I'm not strong enough?"

Aleah makes an air raspberry with her full lips, flapping one hand at me, the wide sleeve of her dark blue dress carrying her spicy scent to me. "No fear of that, love," she says. "Not even a little."

Nice to know someone thinks I can do it. Even if the seed of doubt Bianca planted digs in a bit deeper and sulks.

I hate to let her ruin it for me. And maybe having doubt is a good thing, will keep me grounded. Because I never, ever want to be like her.

"Now," Aleah grabs my arm and pulls me toward the kitchen. "It's time to toss you to the lions and see if I'm right."

"Sorry?" I go with her, choiceless, though I would have gone anyway had she asked. Would have done anything she wanted after that talk. But when I see Piper across the room, hear his squeal of excitement, I freeze.

He runs toward me, a huge smile on his face. Pushes the magazine he's holding into my hands. It's *Backstage*, the newest edition.

And a paragraph is circled in red pen.

"My darling Skyley," Aleah says in her rich voice, "we're sending you on your first audition."

# Chapter Fourteen

My first instinct is panic. Second is disbelief. Third is horror as the magazine begins to tremble in my hands.

"You're crazy," I say. "I can't audition for anything." I need more classes, have to go to school.

Don't I?

Piper snorts, smacks my shoulder. "Don't be a pussy," he says. "Besides, we're all here to help you."

Not all. I can feel Bianca's eyes boring holes in my head. And thank her as her negative attention straightens my spine, gives me the little surge of temper I need to see this through.

"Let's do it," I say.

I'm swept into a whirlwind of activity when they find out I'm not only without a resume, but I also don't have a current headshot. Miller dives for his laptop, hunching over the keyboard with eager fingers. As I dictate my feeble acting experience—though I refuse to look at Bianca, knowing she's probably smirking and rolling her eyes—Aleah seats me on a stool and proceeds to do my hair and makeup.

I catch a quick look at myself in the window beside me, but that's all she allows before Piper spins me around, my back to the brick wall, an expensive looking camera in his hands.

"Don't stress, darling," he says as he lifts it to look at me through the lens. "It's a tiny little production."

"The perfect place for you to get your feet wet," Aleah says, hovering in the background as the rest of our friends call out suggestions for poses and Miller smiles and types.

I feel uncomfortable at first, but soon relax into the experience when I realize Piper won't stop snapping pictures until I do. "If you say so." I try a small smile, thinking of Delores and her sultry yet broken soul. To which my photographer squeals.

"Gorgeous!" He snaps another. "More like that."

Aleah, meanwhile, is on the phone. "Yes, my name is Riley James." She winks at me as I gape at her. "That's right, for the part of Beatrix. Yes. 8pm tomorrow? Perfect. Thank you." And hangs up with a tight smirk.

I choke out a laugh, Piper still snapping away. "Thank you," I say.

Piper is suddenly done, Aleah and Miller both hanging over the back of the camera, oohing and ahhing over shots. But when I try to see, my actor turned photographer jerks the camera away.

"Not a chance," Piper says. "You'll see them when they are printed."

"No fair." I reach for the camera, only to have Aleah block me, wagging one finger in my face.

"Trust us," she says. "Remember?"

It's clear they have no intention of allowing me to interfere. Makes me wonder just what Miller wrote on my resume.

Piper disappears into a corner with a cable and

his own computer, the light from the screen making him look like a mad scientist as he giggles and scowls and sighs over the shots he took. Aleah doesn't allow me to focus on him, doing everything she can to distract me while Piper presumably attempts choose a headshot that meets his approval.

I give in with a shrug and wipe the lipstick from my mouth as Miller hands me a cooler.

"Proud of you," he says.

I'm kind of proud of me, too.

I don't get a chance to enjoy my drink, one sip enough to wash the taste of lipstick from my mouth before I'm firmly taken by the hand and planted in front of the entire group. Aleah claps her hands for attention. I glance around, happy to see Bianca is gone, though Ruben looks sour, staring into his drink. She must have abandoned him when she left.

I'm frankly glad she's gone. Because Aleah spins to face everyone as they sink to the floor in a semi-circle before me and fall quiet.

"Now," she says, turning to me. "Show us your audition."

And leaves me there to stutter and stammer while my new friends laugh.

"That won't get you far," Miller says to more laughter.

"I don't know," Latanya, one of the other girls, says. Her long, black braids hang to her waist, skin darker than Aleah's, eyes sparkling with good humor. "I kind of liked it. Shows originality in nerves."

They can stop laughing any time now.

And since I realize they aren't going to let me off the hook anytime soon, I choose to be brave and launch into one of my monologues.

It's hard, at first, to find the place I need to be

inside myself and I stumble through the words, the phrasing, the timing. My friends don't comment until I'm done, though the critiques come hard and fast once I've fallen silent.

I listen, absorb what they say. "Too stiff" "Breathe already" "More movement" and take it all in. Before trying again.

This time the quiet comes more easily, the detachment, now I've lost the edge to my nerves. Though I still struggle to leave room open for the return of the character. Yet, it's easier than ever to fall into the stillness and allow the voice to flow, but I know I'm missing a piece.

I need more practice.

This time, the group's comments are more positive.

I spend the next few hours working hard, finding the place I need to be in the character, expanding on my audition to a soft song of loss I've taken from a small show I did in high school. I have a half-decent voice, though I'm no Aleah. Still, they applaud and offer more suggestions while I sigh in happiness.

They finally leave me be, hugs coming from all sides, even Ruben giving me a squeeze and a "great job" in my ear. Piper bounces around like a manic two-year-old, hugging me after Ruben lets me go.

Hands me a sticky note. Actually adheres it to my arm. "Pick up your photos tomorrow," he says. "They'll be ready by five."

My nerves return, though I trust him as he hugs me again.

"Thank you." I've been saying that a lot to these people I now call my friends.

Piper waves one hand in front of his face, lower lip trembling. "You hush," he says. "An ugly cry will ruin my mascara."

I kiss his cheek. "Can't have that," I say.

Aleah is next. "Well done," she says. "I can't wait to see you on stage."

A thrill of excitement goes through me even as I feel my phone vibrate in my pocket. I fish it out, grinning at her.

See the reminder I left myself earlier to go home and get some sleep.

And sigh at the order. Know I need to, now more than ever.

More hugs, goodbyes for everyone. I'm at the elevator when Miller stops me. He leans against the wall, soft smile impossible not to adore. "You know you can say no, right?" He gestures behind him. "If you think you're not ready."

Does he doubt me? That hurts, almost as much as Bianca's little bitch fest. "No," I say. Pause because I trust his judgment. "Do you think I should?"

Miller laughs and kisses my cheek. "Are you kidding?" His finger traces over my jaw, a feather touch I have to fight not to lean into. "I'm the one who suggested the audition."

Restoring my faith and wiping away the pain with a few simple words.

"I can't let you walk home alone." He straightens even as Aleah and Piper, a few of the others tagging along, head for us. Aleah takes my hand.

"Sushi run," she says. "Sure you can't stay?"

I shake my head, smile at Miller. "I think I'll be okay."

I feel as disappointed as he looks when he nods. But now there's no way to ask him to come with me, not when Aleah is on one side, Piper on the other, the elevator door sliding shut on Miller's wave goodbye.

Probably just as well. Since we're friends and all. Nothing more than friends.

*Am I ready to make it more?*

The streets are as quiet as New York is going to

get, though Aleah makes short work of that. She bursts into song as we walk, Piper joining her, Latanya and Malik, her delicious, dark-haired boyfriend, join in. They must have been in a show together, no way such a sound could be improvised. Doesn't stop me from trying to find a part to sing among their voices.

At first it's odd, I'm only humming, Aleah smiling at me as she sings. But, like magic, my mind clicks and everything fits together. I can almost see the line of harmony, dive into it with enthusiasm, though I'm still humming because I don't know the words.

As we near Aunt Vonda's, I look up at the roof and laugh, breaking my own concentration. I wanted to be part of this, longed for exactly what I'm doing right now.

Amazing what a few days and some courage can do.

I wave goodbye to my friends, who serenade me all the way to the door of the building, around 1AM. Blow them kisses, laughing, heart so full I'm sure I won't sleep after all. But when the entry closes behind me and I'm engulfed by quiet, I feel my body finally ready to quit and know sleeping won't be a problem.

As I fall into bed, I smile at Ian's picture. Touch his image held behind the glass. Strangely, I don't feel the need to call up more than that.

And think of Miller.

# Chapter Fifteen

Aunt Vonda is so excited the next morning when I tell her what I have planned, she spills her tea all over the table. I accept her hug with one of my own, though I'm beginning to think if the people who love me don't stop choking me, I won't be around much longer.

She sits back, clapping like a crazy lady, red-tinted curls barely moving as she bounces in her seat.

"Riley," she gushes all over me, "that's so wonderful!"

We walk together to work, my few hours of sleep enough to keep my spirits up, tied to the excitement of knowing tomorrow night I'll be auditioning for my first real show. My first New York show.

It's hard to focus on flowers and customer's orders, especially when Aunt Vonda proceeds to inform anyone who will listen I'm going to be a famous actress someday. When I'm not blushing furiously and hissing at her to be quiet, I'm giggling behind my hands in giddy half-hysteria at the thought she might be right.

I'm actually disappointed when Miller and Aleah, Piper in tow, don't appear at all during the day. I was so sure they would come to see me. But I end up shaking my head at myself, settling my nerves and my excitement. Silly, I'd be seeing them later.

For more rehearsals.

I'm shocked when I slip out of the back from a short break to the sound of the doorbell, look up, and find Bianca standing at the counter. My whole body shudders, zinging pops of pinpoint needles racing down my limbs at the sight of her. I realize then I'm afraid of her, intimidated.

And no matter what I do to shake off the feeling, I can't seem to manage it.

But Aunt Vonda is gone and there is no one else to serve her. I feel my cheeks heat as I walk to the counter, oddly embarrassed Bianca is seeing me like this. Self-conscious, smoothing the front of my pink apron even as I wonder if I look like crap and hate that I care. I meet Bianca's eyes.

Expecting a bitch to stare back at me. Some harsh words, bitterness. Instead, she smiles at me, full of charm and charisma, leaning over the counter to squeeze my wrist as though she didn't do her damnedest last night to squash my heart and stomp on it with her high heels.

"Riley," she says in her sultry voice. "I'm so happy you're here."

She is? I stiffen as she pulls back, blonde hair rippling. She looks flawless, perfection, exactly how a New York actor should look. And I'm all frumpy in my stained pink apron and hair haphazardly hanging from the messy knot at my neck.

Bianca's smile fades a little as she rests her manicured hands on the counter. "I wanted to apologize," she says. "For last night. Thank you for coming to my show."

I know I'm staring and look like she just hit me, but I can't seem to call up much more than that. Is she bipolar? Has an evil twin?

"You really did make an impression last night," she goes on. "That street scene of yours... it's nice to see Miller acting again. Since all the trouble."

Trouble? "He's incredible," I say. Whisper, actually.

Another flash of smile. "He really is," she says. "I just wish he'd decide if we're on again or off again." She tosses those words at me with a regretful smile even as my stomach plummets.

"You're together?" Why didn't he tell me that?

*Because, we're friends, not dating, so he didn't have to tell me anything. And I'm an idiot. Of course someone as beautiful as Miller is with Bianca.*

The disappointment bites deep, though I think I do a great job not showing it. Hope I do. I don't want her to see how much knowing this hurts me.

Ian's memory calls and I let him appear behind her, scowling down at her when I can't, when I'm forced—by my own sheer refusal to give in to my pain—to just nod when she shrugs.

"Honestly, he's been such a train wreck the last year or so," she says, rolling her eyes, voice dropping into a "just us girls" tone. "I guess I saw you with him and was feeling a teensy weensy jealous." She laughs then. "Silly, right?"

I nod, numb. "Very," I say. "Miller is just a friend."

She leans against the counter, head cocked to one side, blue eyes batting lashes at me. "You do know everything I said last night was meant with heart, right?" She pouts a little. "I didn't mean to be harsh. But this is a tough business and I've seen so many girls stumble and fall."

I know she's playing me, feel it in my soul, but I

want to believe her, pulled in by her charisma and the fact she's who I want to be. Well, at least, she's where I want to be.

"Thanks," I say. "I know it's tough. I watched my mother go through it."

Why did I say that? Because I want her to know. I want to impress Bianca, drop Mom's name. *What is wrong with me?* It's like I need her approval when every bone in my body vibrates with instructions to back away from her and not listen.

From the slight narrowing of Bianca's eyes, I realize she already knows who I am. "Yes," she says. "I have to say, I had no idea Marie St. Claire even had a daughter." She flashes her teeth. "You certainly look very much like her."

I absorb her antagonism, thinly veiled now behind her veneer of big sister concern and feel my stomach coil into the tightest knot I've ever experienced. This is surreal and painful as Bianca straightens, tosses her blonde hair in her favorite move and shrugs.

"I'm sure you'll do fine," she says. Turns to go. Pauses, blue eyes staring over her shoulder at me. "I just wanted to touch base. In case you needed anything." She taps her fingers on the strap of her purse. "You're new to the group. Maybe you can keep an eye on Miller for me. To make sure he's not backsliding."

"Into what?" Oh, the train wreck she mentioned. I'm curious despite myself, despite the need to shove her out of the store and into the street and slam the door in her face. Ian continues to hover, to glare as Bianca's lips turn down.

"Just…" She stops. Tinkles a laugh. "I'm sorry," she says, rueful smile under her hard, glittering eyes. "His drug use isn't your problem."

She leaves as the doorbell rings and a man in a suit enters. I watch her sashay her way out, hips swaying to a slow, sexy beat. My customer's eyes lift from her ass to mine and he clears his throat.

It's not until I've served him, handed him his change, alone again in the shop, I realize my phantom summoning of Ian is gone.

My heart beats way too fast.

Aunt Vonda bustles back in, dropping the keys to the van on the counter, patting my hand. "Thanks for holding down the fort," she says.

I bob a nod, pull myself together. Smile even, when another customer arrives. I sort flowers for a small spring bouquet and tell myself it's not only none of my business Miller and Bianca are a couple but that his drug problem—whatever that means— really doesn't have anything to do with me.

By the time Melissa, Aunt Vonda's part-timer, arrives to take over for me at five o'clock, I've convinced myself both are true.

I wait for my aunt to finish before heading home. With a purposeful detour. I'm nervous about the headshots, and I want her with me to see them.

It's only another two blocks to the printer. The smiling girl behind the counter retrieves my photos when I tell her my name.

I turn to Aunt Vonda and hand her the thick envelop of 8X11's. "I can't look."

She practically rips the flap off in her haste, slips one of the images free even as the clerk says, "You're very photogenic." Aunt Vonda's huge eyes and gasp of surprise makes me finally duck around her and peek.

"Marie," Aunt Vonda whispers, voice rough. "Riley, pet. You look just like your mother."

I stare at myself, at the masterpiece my friends made for me, and feel near to tears myself. My fingers shake as I take the slick photo from her, looking down at my face. Piper's photo perfecting skills are clearly formidable. My skin is flawless, the makeup Aleah applied so seamlessly it has to have been altered. By the time I arrived home last night and looked in the mirror, I was a fright of stress-rubbed eye shadow and sweat-streaked foundation topped by my messy hair.

Aleah had worked a miracle with a flat iron on my natural waves, giving me a bouncy curl at the ends, sweeping my bangs in a wave of awesome. I wish I looked like that all the time. I can hardly believe it's me but for the large "Riley James" written in the bottom right corner.

When I flip it over, I realize Miller had my resume printed on the back. Aunt Vonda notices at the same time. We shuffle to the side to allow the next customer by and hunch together in the quiet store to read it, me as much in awe of his words as my aunt.

"He makes you sound so professional," she says even as I gape at the description of my acting experience.

I pause part way and have to stop. "I just did some school and community theater," I say over the glowing words he used. "This is…"

"Perfect." Aunt Vonda squeezes my arm and slips hers through. I replace the picture with her help before accepting the sleeve of photos and leaving the store with her, still stunned.

I just hope this little charade my friends are creating won't get me into trouble.

I can barely eat dinner, already planning to head out to Miller's for rehearsal. Aunt Vonda chatters away and I'm grateful for her conversational skills. I barely have to nod and murmur agreement to keep her happy. I know it isn't fair, but she doesn't seem to mind.

I'm heading for the door, my purse over my shoulder, when the phone rings. Aunt Vonda answers, while I slip on my sandals, mind already on the street, on Aleah and Piper. A flare of brief pain when I think of Miller.

Squashed when I consider I'm about to rehearse for my first audition.

"Yes. She's here. Just a moment." I turn to see Aunt Vonda's face scrunched into unhappiness. She covers the receiver with her hand, mouths, "your father," at me.

The last person I want to talk to right now.

"Riley, pet," she whispers. "I'm so sorry. I emailed him to tell him how excited I was for you." Her distress is still growing even as I feel like she's just punched me in the stomach. "I should have left it to you." Aunt Vonda winces. "I'll tell him I missed you."

I shake my head, reach for the phone. "It's okay," I say, registering the dull, dead tone of my voice, furious I've lost my excitement in the sinking feeling I have whenever I think about Dad. "He would have found out eventually anyway." I'm really not in the mood for a lecture, but putting Dad off will just make things worse later.

Aunt Vonda sighs sadly and hands over the phone. I take a breath, go over the talk I had with Aleah last night. Focus on how acting makes me feel.

And instantly perk as I say, "Hi, Dad."

"Your aunt seems to think you've decided to start acting." His cold tone vibrates with anger, his wording so reminiscent of Bianca's first words to me my temper crackles. I know that tone. Have been on the other side of it most of my life, only this time he's really pissed.

"I'm auditioning for a show tomorrow," I say, keeping my own voice light as I repeat a mantra in my head and decide not to engage him no matter how much I want to let loose my anger.

*Remember how it feels. Remember how it feels.*

"What the hell are you thinking?" Dad blows much more quickly than I'm used to. "I told Vonda no acting. You're supposed to be making money for college, not hanging out with losers and wasting time on stupid theater."

I don't comment, struggling to cling to the scene on the street as my temper fires off.

"I gave you leeway when Ian was alive," Dad says, voice dropping again, ice cold and full of fury, "but it's time to grow the hell up. Either you give up this ridiculousness, or you get your ass back home."

Delores hums in the back of my head, the character reminding me why I'm even willing to argue with him. "Mom wanted me to act," I say, heat finally breaking through my tone. "And so did Ian."

Dad's silence is so long I think maybe he's hung up. Until he speaks again.

"They're dead," he snaps. "Both of them. And I'm your father."

I almost say, "So?" But hold my tongue.

"You're making a fool of yourself." Dad's voice shakes, and I can picture him standing in the kitchen at home, hand fisted on the counter, face a black cloud of doom and anger. "And I won't have it. There's no future for you in acting. You need to get your priorities straight or I'll do it for you."

My thumb hits the end key before my brain realizes I've hung up on him.

I stand there for a long moment, staring at the phone as though Dad is going to magically appear through it. The world shakes as my anger recedes and I turn. Hand the phone back to Aunt Vonda. Her eyes are wet with tears, cheeks pale as she reaches for me with one hand. I dodge her, shrug Dad off. Head for my room instead of out the door.

Close myself into my little oasis as my brain

explodes with anger.

# Chapter Sixteen

I need to go to Miller's, but I can't bring myself to leave. I pace my room, fury driving my stomping steps around the end of my bed to the window and back again.

My phone vibrates. I check the message, expecting a hateful note from Dad, only to see Susan's smiling icon staring back at me.

I call, on impulse, sink to the edge of the bed, still shaking.

She answers right away. "Riley!" She sounds happy for once. "Sorry to bug you, honey. I just wanted to check in and see how you were."

I sob in frustration, hear her soothing croon on the other end of the line, gasp an apology. "I'm fine," I finally say, wiping my nose on the back of my hand before reaching for a tissue when I realize I'm a slimy mess. "It's just Dad."

She listens as I rage about him, up and pacing all over again. By the time I'm sitting once more, my anger has dissipated somewhat, though my determination to tell him to piss off hasn't gone anywhere.

"Your father loves you," Susan says while I snort my disbelief. "He does, in his own way." Her sigh is heavy, sounds like static. "But he's wrong. You're so talented, Rye. And you need to be acting.

Ian knew it. And Dwight and I know it, too. You're a natural."

At least someone approves. I correct myself, Aunt Vonda has been wonderful. My new friends. "I just wish he wasn't such a…"

Asshole seems too mild a word.

"I don't understand Rick's problem," Susan says, soft and kind. "But I know he wants what's best for you." She lets that sink in while I fume. "But you're a grown woman now, honey. And you need to do what makes you happy."

"Even if it pisses Dad off?"

Susan sighs again. "Even if," she says. "Riley, we are so proud of you. You are the most beautiful, courageous, strong young woman we know. If Ian had lived…" she goes quiet a moment, I know she's pulling herself together, "we would have been delighted to have you as our daughter-in-law. But he didn't. So we have to be satisfied in loving you as the daughter we never had."

I want to cry all over again, this time in gratitude. "Thanks, Susan," I say. "I love you both so much."

"Now," she says, sniffing softly as though trying to hide it from me. "You let us know the minute the audition is over. I want to celebrate."

She's assuming I'll get the part. A crooked grin lifts my lips and my spirits. "Will do."

We part with more I love you's. When I set down the phone, I'm calmer, ready to face whatever comes.

A soft knock on the door raises my head, Aunt Vonda's nervous face poking in.

"Are you okay, pet?" She looks so upset, I offer my hand to her. She enters immediately, sits beside me, trembling hands patting my knee. "I'm so sorry, Riley. He's such an ass sometimes. And I should have minded my own damned business instead of trying to make that stupid oaf admit he's wrong to be so hard on you."

I almost qualify her "sometimes" with "all the time", but don't bother. "It's really okay, Aunt Vonda," I say. "I'm glad you broke it to him." I am, too. Yes, the call was unpleasant. But it's over and I'm moving forward. "I'm going to do it anyway."

She smiles, tentative and anxious. "I'm so glad." One more pat to my knee and she relaxes.

"I just wish I knew why he can't love me," I say, verbalizing the question for the first time, amazing myself I even bother to ask. I've never spoken of it, told myself I didn't care. But I obviously do from the lump rising in my throat. "He treats me like I'm a mistake."

All our years alone together, after Mom's death, pile on top of me in layers, suffocating, smothering me.

Aunt Vonda shakes her head, clutches my hand in hers, pulling me loose from my own oppression, helping me breathe again. "No, pet," she says. "Not a mistake at all. I think, because you remind him so much of Marie, he has a hard time with the hurt he still carries. I know he doesn't mean to be cruel to you. But he's never gotten over your mother's loss. And in such a tragic way."

I swallow the grief rising from my chest. "If only she hadn't gotten sick," I say, remembering the night Dad came to my room. Hovered at the door. Told me Mom had a sudden illness and she was dead, just like that. His dull and lifeless voice, the first time he felt like a stranger to me. He's been a stranger ever since.

Aunt Vonda's sudden frown makes me frown, too.

"Sick?" She seems shocked, angry, so angry all of a sudden I worry her temper is aimed at me. "Who told you your mother died of an illness?"

Her words are a slap across my face. I don't

answer. I don't have to. Her fury turns to denial and then to guilt tinged with bubbling rage.

"Richard Morris James." She mutters Dad's full name, hands still trembling, but two hot points of red stand out on her cheekbones, mottled pink crawling down her neck and over her chest as her unhappiness simmers. Her eyes meet mine, snapping with temper. "He told you your mother... Oh, Riley. Pet, this is my fault. I should have been there for you."

"Aunt Vonda." I'm proud of how steady my voice is, how calm I feel despite the fact I now know the explanation Dad gave me that night, to a little girl waiting for her mother, wasn't true. My aunt's reaction tells me as much. "What happened to my mother?"

Aunt Vonda shifts on the bed beside me, as though suddenly nervous, though her anger remains. "Rick fell in love with Marie from the moment they met," she says, ignoring my question, her words tumbling out of her mouth as though she's been trying to decide what to say to me for years. "I remember the first time I met her, thinking she was more alive than he was. More than any of us." Aunt Vonda's fingers tighten. "Not in an arrogant way. Just that she shone so much brighter. Everyone loved her. She was a star, even before she was a professional actress." She slumps beside me. "I loved her, too. I idolized her, Riley." That word makes me think of Bianca. "But my brother adored her and would do anything for her. He used to laugh, at least a little, when Marie was alive. When they were first together." One hand rises to wipe at her eye as a tear falls. "He had so much trouble showing his emotions. Our father wasn't the kindest man, and Rick took after him." I don't remember my grandfather, who died before I was born. "But when Marie was around, my brother was a different person."

So difficult for me to believe. And yet, not so much. I recall moments of happiness with the three of us, seeing Dad smile, though the memories are dim and warped. It's so long ago and I've pushed that part of my history under my current feelings for him. I guess I didn't want to remember.

"Marie shone and your father was happy to be in the background, cheering her on. But love, pet. Sometimes love just isn't enough." She takes my hands in hers.

Do I want to know what she's about to tell me? Panic surges, fights for the air in my lungs, for my heartbeat. I'm immobilized by it, forced to listen no matter my desires yea or nay.

"Marie was a wonderful person," Aunt Vonda says. "I don't ever want you to think otherwise. She loved you and your father. But when you're young, just starting out, things appear one way. All fresh and full of possibility. Then when we start to grow up..." she releases my hands, hers falling into the lap of her blue dress, her eyes downcast. "We can grow apart from those we used to want to spend the rest of our lives with."

My mother...

"Riley," Aunt Vonda says, "your father lied to you, maybe to protect you. Maybe to protect himself. But your mother didn't die of an illness. She died in a car accident." Her jaw jumps. "With the man she loved."

# Chapter Seventeen

Even as I battle denial and anger, the image of a smiling man rises in my mind. I barely remember him, but he wasn't Dad. Mom introduced us, one day at the park. He drove us around in his shiny convertible and bought me ice cream. I remember wondering why Mom smiled so much.

"How could she do that?" It's weird for me to take Dad's side, especially considering he never has taken mine. But I always thought my parents were happy. Until I came along. I blamed Dad's hate for me on myself, never knowing it was Mom's infidelity that drove the wedge between Dad and me.

Aunt Vonda looked away, cheeks wet with tears. "Everyone makes mistakes," she says. "And sometimes you can love someone, but that love doesn't last, for one reason or another." Her fingers twist together in her lap. "I lost my Sal to a stroke far too young. He was only thirty-eight, you know." I nod, empathy for her instantly smothering my anger. "He left me with two kids and a business to run." She pats my hand again as though the gesture will make everything all right.

"I understand your loss, pet," she says. "How much Ian meant to you. Maybe that loss can help you see how your father reacted the way he did. How it broke his heart and wouldn't allow him to love you for fear he'd shatter and not be able to put himself back together."

I bite my lip. I can't go there. I think Aunt Vonda knows it, because she goes on.

"I don't want you to judge your mother. Neither of us went through what she did. " Aunt Vonda shakes her head. "Your mother moved on, forced by her career. And she fell out of love with Rick because she outgrew him. It happens, Riley. It's not nice, and maybe it's not fair. But it does happen." She pauses. "I know how this sounds. Like Marie chose her career, the stage, over you and your father. But that's not true at all. She would never put anyone or anything before you."

I can't help but feel betrayed no matter what Aunt Vonda says. "She was going to divorce Dad." I don't know why I feel numb from the knowledge. Lots of people break up these days. It's just I've lived a lie my whole life, and now I'm trying to figure out who my father is. Who my mother was. And who I am because of them and the choices they made.

"I guess I shouldn't be surprised Rick lied to you," Aunt Vonda says with a new edge to her voice as she swipes at her cheeks with one hand. "He never wanted to admit Marie was having an affair."

It does explain a great deal to me, though. About how Dad treats me. "He must hate me for reminding him of Mom," I say.

And blames acting for his wife's infidelity.

My temper blazes to life and I surge to my feet, pacing to the end of the bed, to the window. I stare out, hands clenched at my sides, furious with both of them. At Mom for dying, for cheating on Dad. At my father for punishing me for something I couldn't change. At myself for allowing him to hurt me over and over again because he didn't have the balls to tell me the truth.

The twelve-year-old girl inside me, the one who lost her mother, cries as my anger peaks. I thought my mother was sick. Died suddenly of heart failure because of illness. While all along it was my father's heart that failed.

I turn back to Aunt Vonda to see her watching me with nervous sadness of her own.

"You need to live your own life, pet," she says. "Not the one Rick seems to think is good for you." She hurries on before I can reply. "You've inspired me," she says, a smile taking the place of her frown of guilt and grief. "To try new things. I need to go out there and just take that damned pottery class." She stomps one foot, breaks my mood and I catch myself smiling over her expression of determination. I'm grateful as she continues for helping me wiggle out from under all my own pain for a moment. "I've always wanted to," Aunt Vonda says, hands wringing with clear anxiety. "But I'm afraid."

My eyebrows shoot up. "You're afraid?" I find that so hard to believe. The aunt I know has always been a powerhouse, boisterous and charismatic, a widowed mother raising my cousins with a smile and always with a ready hug for me.

Aunt Vonda's nose scrunches as she comes around the end of the bed and across the room to stand in front of me. "I know what I look like on the outside." She pats her hair, a funny physical tic I never noticed until I moved here. "But I've had to show my confident side. I've had to step up, out of need, not natural ability. Or I never would have been able to run the business, take care of the kids, go on without Sal." She steps in and hugs me and I hug her back. "I know flowers," she says. "But I don't know courage, not anymore. I've allowed myself to fall into the same old thing, day in and day out." She leans away, smiles up at me. "Trying new things for fun—not out of necessity—has always made me nervous."

I'm learning so much about the people in my life today.

"Now," she says, letting her hands fall away from me, smile widening, "I'm signed up for tomorrow night. And I'm going." A quick bob of her head, narrowing of her eyes.

I love my Aunt Vonda.

She hugs me when I grab her this time. "You're awesome," I say, thinking of Piper and how he's so right, the night of that first class, when he told me I was awesome no matter what.

She giggles in my ear, but steps away again, sobering. "No matter your mother's issues," she says, "or your father's, you inherited Marie's talent. Use it. And don't let anyone keep you from it."

Aunt Vonda leaves my room, closing the door softly behind her. I sit on the end of the bed, still at odds with the lie that's been my life, unable to generate the energy to hate either one of my parents anymore.

One thing I'm sure of, though. I'm not my mother. Her image is now far too close to Bianca's for my liking and I shy from that comparison. I was right to tell Miller not to say anything about being the daughter of Marie St. Clair, and I doubt Bianca will have a reason to bring it up. I don't want to use my mother's reputation, fly on her coattails.

I have my own future to create. One where I make the right choices.

Now, if only I can figure out what the right choices look like...

Sighing out my frustration and finally deciding I've had enough family drama, I grab my purse and head for Miller's. To hide in my one true love and see if I can find it in me to forgive my parents for all the hurt I've lived in the last nine years.

Maybe, just maybe, I can then prove to Dad I'm not my mother.

# Chapter Eighteen

I stand on the street, gathering my courage and doing my best to keep my heart from pounding out of my chest. All of my confidence from the last two days of rehearsals seems to have left me in a rush, the moment my eyes landed on the address Piper handed me just an hour ago.

"Break a leg," he said. Hugged me. I know he wanted to come, but Aleah's suggestion it would be better for me if the entire gang wasn't hanging out in the place watching me made sense. Yes, they'd been there all along, but I'm thinking in a live action situation, their focus and attention might be more harm than help.

I've never been hugged so many times in such a short span, finally spinning into the elevator alone.

Aleah, Miller, and Piper waved goodbye to me as the doors closed and I headed for home to shower and change for my audition. Bless Aunt Vonda for giving me the afternoon off to keep rehearsing. I think she's still troubled by Dad's lie about Mom. Though a few hours rehearsing the same night I found out helped me shunt it off to a corner and ignore it for a little while.

I just want to forget and focus on my future.

My excitement held through my shower, through carefully dressing in the simple blue sheath and shrug sweater, high heeled sandals, barely there makeup and no jewelry. Hair swept back from my face so the director can see me. I followed all the rules my friends laid out to optimize my chances for casting. I liked what I saw in my bathroom mirror.

Ian lay on the bed, conjured by my nerves and my need to just have him with me. I'd been doing so less frequently lately, not craving his constant presence, and his form wavered before I lost him and let him go.

I try not to be troubled by the fact I'm actually moving on.

I feel like I have no troubles at all as I stride down the street, bag over my shoulder, precious headshot in a folder tucked inside. Zero nerves until I see that door, the address above it.

And realize this isn't just some game, some fantasy. It's very real.

I'm about to audition for my first official show and I'm suddenly terrified.

My phone hums, grabs my attention. I fish it out, check the text from Aunt Vonda.

*So proud of you, pet.*

Tears spike in my eyes, stinging. I bite my lower lip as I text back a smiley face, the best I can manage.

Look up at the door. Draw a deep breath. It's show time.

When I open the door, the space is cool at least, the city's heavy at the beginning of a heat wave. The tiny beads of sweat I didn't notice on my skin outside now make me shiver in the air conditioning as my skin erupts into goosebumps. I pass through the tiny lobby when a young man behind the ticket counter waves me on. He must know why I'm here.

Why am I here again?

The doors to the theater are open and, as I pass through them, my nerves suddenly lessen. This is a very small venue, maybe fifty seats. Nothing like the large theater where I watched Bianca's show the other night. Something about knowing there will be fewer people in the audience makes me feel better.

So does the sight of Aleah and Miller sitting off to one side. They weren't going to come, they promised they wouldn't. But I'm so happy to see them I head to greet them, trembling like a leaf under a stiff wind.

"We'll leave if you want," Aleah says instantly even as she hugs me. I shake my head while Miller takes his turn. I draw great comfort from both of them, mostly from the power of Miller's hug, the way his lips tuck against my ear for a whispered, "you're beautiful," before he lets me go. His close familiarity I've managed to pass off as friendliness, knowing now he's with Bianca. The truth of the situation can still make me sad if I let it.

Not tonight. At least, not now.

"No, please stay." Do I sound desperate? I laugh, trying to take the edge off.

They both chuckle softly and I'm suddenly mindful of the auditions going on at the stage and the volume of my voice. "It's natural to be nervous," Miller says. "Just use it." I look in his eyes and feel the need to talk to him, to ask him about Bianca, his relationship. So odd how I'm losing Ian because of Miller only to understand I can't have him.

Makes me think of Mom and Dad.

I shrug off my parents, Miller and Bianca. It's none of my business.

This audition is.

I turn, look down the aisle toward the small cluster of people sitting on the other side near the front. All girls, like me. Waiting their turn, I suppose. It's odd to think I'm one of them. I knew I wasn't the only one, but it's still weird to see them, to know I'm in competition for this role.

"I know most of them," Aleah whispers in my ear. "Not a speck of talent among them. You'll be fine."

Nice of her to say so. I do relax a little though, reach out and squeeze her hand. "I'll just do my best," I say. "And we'll go from there."

The pretty brunette on stage finishes her audition. I haven't heard a word she said, I'm so nervous. I'm about to join the other girls, glancing at my phone to check the time, when I hear someone laugh at the back, looking up as Bianca, Ruben trailing along with her, struts through the doors.

Aleah's gasp, Miller's soft curse, tells me this is a problem. Bianca glances our way, meets my eyes with a surly smirk, all of her false friendliness gone, before approaching the director. Holds out her arms to him as he surges to his feet and hugs her.

I watch, stomach knotting, as she kisses both of his cheeks. Somehow, I get the feeling she's not here to tell him he should cast me in the role.

Reinforced when I catch her words, "Love to audition," as she pulls away from him. Looks at me again.

Smiles.

Aleah curses softly under her breath, loud enough I hear the odd swear through her rant. Miller grasps my arm, pulls me tight against him.

"Listen to me," he says, voice low and humming with anger. Is he mad at me? Or her? "She's just another person. She's nothing to you. Your audition is all that matters."

Her then. I can't help but think, "Yeah, right." I know I've failed already. Even as Bianca sways her way onto the stage, blonde hair swinging in curls around her, and delivers a flawless audition.

She makes me tremble. Sigh. I want to weep, and that's just her performance. By the time she's done, descending to hug the director again, I've already quit.

And I hate myself for it.

I stay where I am, knowing I'm pale. I probably look like someone just hit me with a truck. I can barely breathe as Bianca leaves the director, Ruben still behind her, and approaches us.

She stops right in front of me, crosses her arms over her chest, one foot tapping on the ground while Aleah and Miller close in around me. Ruben looks embarrassed and won't meet my eyes as Bianca tosses her hair. "Hey there, Riley," she says with her nasty smile. "I didn't know you'd be here tonight."

Ruben twitches. She's such a liar.

"What the hell is wrong with you?" Aleah speaks before Bianca can and I watch the spark of anger trace over the beautiful blonde's face in answer to being beaten to the punch.

"I have no idea what you're talking about." I know she's aiming for a hit, but Aleah's anger seems to have shoved Bianca into a pouting corner. "Now that I've shown little Miss Riley James here how it's done, I'm sure she'll be just fine." Her smile turns to a head-tilt and an eyelash bat. "Won't you, Riley?"

"You know exactly what she's talking about," Miller hisses. He moves to confront Bianca, leaning close to her so I can barely hear. "This little show is too small for your massive ego," he says, lips by her ear. "You're just being a bitch to prove some damned point only you seem to think is important." He backs away from her, face a mask of disapproval. "Get over yourself for once, Bee. For God's sake."

She snarls at him, pushes him away. "Fuck off, Miller," she says.

The only part of this that I can even remotely see as helpful is his reaction to her. That's not the face of a man who loves a woman.

Did she lie about them, to hurt me? I don't have the focus to think it through. My head is spinning.

"I thought you were one of us," Aleah says, voice cold. "My mistake."

"It's a free world," Bianca snarls back. "And the director is a friend." We noticed. "Besides, if you're that worried your pathetic little small town can't compete, she shouldn't be here."

Tosses her head again, glares at me. And then smiles one last time.

"Good luck," she says, rolling her eyes as she turns away. Ruben continues to look down and when Bianca takes his arm, he hesitates. But he leaves with her and I wonder if Piper knows his boyfriend is a traitor asshole.

Aleah grabs my upper arms, shakes me. "Do not let her ruin this," she says.

I nod. But it's over already.

I go through the motions because Aleah and Miller want me to. I walk over to sit with the other girls. The auditions are running late. There are several actors ahead of me. I feel myself sinking further into my seat as they audition, knowing they are better than me. That Bianca is better than me. *Why am I here? This is crazy. I'm not ready and I never will be.*

When the director calls my name, I almost don't hear him. Glancing up when he repeats it, I see Bianca sitting behind him. I slip my headshot from the folder, hand it to his assistant who looks irritated at the delay. And drag myself, a step at a time, to the stage.

I turn and look out over the auditorium, empty but for three girls waiting to audition after me. Miller and Aleah in the back. And the director, Bianca behind him, whispering together. Looking at me. Laughing.

The director rolls his eyes and nods to something she says. I see him set my headshot aside before I've even auditioned. I know what it means, so why bother?

"Anytime," he says, voice bored as Bianca sits back with that same hateful smirk on her face.

I open my mouth, try to find my gift, try so hard to do what Aleah wants, to forget this and just remember the night on the street. My rehearsals. But I can't.

My body, my soul, my heart, all frozen. I can't say a single word.

It feels like forever, though I know it's probably only a few seconds. But my confidence is gone, robbed and I'm done.

The director leans forward with a frown. "You're not Marie St. Claire's daughter," he says. I see Bianca's smile deepen, feel myself shrivel from the association with my mother. "Either audition," he says, "or get the hell off the stage so someone else can."

My feet push me toward the stairs, too fast as I stumble down. I'm already picking up speed, running for the exit, refusing to burst into tears right here, in front of everyone. I manage to hold them in until I hit the street.

But not before I hear the director calling after me, "Thanks for wasting our time, small town."

My hate for Bianca makes me sob into the heat of the New York evening while total strangers step around me, as if afraid my misery is contagious.

# Chapter Nineteen

I know I need to stop crying, but I can't. When I feel hands on my shoulders, I only cry harder. I turn to find Aleah standing there, holding my bag, Miller beside her. They both look so distressed, like this is their fault, I gulp down my tears and shake my head so hard I feel a headache coming on.

And anger.

"Screw her." My voice is louder than I intended. "Screw Bianca and her whole fucking attitude."

Aleah's jaw tightens as she hands me my purse. "I'm sorry, Riley," she says.

I shake my head again, light headed from the abruptness of the motion. "Just never mind," I say. "Never mind any of it." I back away from them, dashing at the tears on my cheeks with angry fingers. "I let her ruin it, didn't I? It's my own fault." I'm such an idiot, a loser. Bianca's right. No amount of loving the job prepared me for this.

*If I can't act under pressure, I might as well quit while I'm ahead.*

Miller tries to follow me, but I take another step back, hold out my hand to stave him off. "I just need to go home." And turn my back on them both.

Head down, hands tight around the strap of my purse, I run away like a coward.

I alternate between hating Bianca and beating the crap out of myself for even trying. In a rush of need, Ian is beside me, my imaginary love keeping pace. I feel his concern for me, his sadness and I embrace it. I just want to crawl into bed next to his phantom and forget the real world even exists.

By the time my shaking fingers shove my key in the lock, I'm ready to pack my bags and return home to Clifton. Bury myself in Ian's memory and never surface again. Dad's right, as much as the truth stabs me in the heart.

Nothing good can come of this.

The moment I walk through the door, Aunt Vonda is there, arms open. We hug and I cry on her shoulder. I don't know how she knows what I need, but she guides me to the kitchen table where a carton of my favorite ice cream and two spoons wait for me.

I sink into the chair, stuffing in a big mouthful of chocolate and slump over, free hand barely able to hold up my head.

Aunt Vonda takes her own bite, silent, but so supportive she almost makes things worse.

"I bombed," I say at last. Ian's ghost settles into the chair next to me, silent and watchful. "No, I didn't even get a chance to bomb. Because I couldn't get a damned word out of my mouth."

Aunt Vonda licks her spoon. "First audition," she says. "You expected anything else?"

I stare at her. "What?"

I wish she wouldn't laugh. It reminds me of Bianca and her fucking smirk.

"Darling pet," Aunt Vonda says. "I remember holding your mother's hand after her first audition while she sobbed her heart out and drank a pint of scotch to try to make herself forget the disaster."

My mother? The director said there was no way I was her daughter. Asshole. What did he know?

Aunt Vonda sets down her spoon. "Everyone starts somewhere," she says. "But not everyone keeps going."

I nod, wonder at my emotional upheaval, why I'm letting this all hurt me so much. I used to be good at staying level, not showing emotion except with Ian. For Ian. *Why is this different?* "Because I want it," I whisper when I understand. Aunt Vonda doesn't say anything. "I guess I just have to toughen up." *When did I become weak, lost, pathetic?*

Aunt Vonda leans toward me, her hand stopping the spoon from taking another scoop of chocolate to my mouth. "It's not about being tough," she says, "or thick skinned. At least, according to your mother." Mom again. I almost pull free of Aunt Vonda's grip, but hold still and make myself listen. "It's about trusting your heart, your passion. And your talent."

If that's the case, I'm totally screwed because I have zippo trust hanging around me at the moment. Only Ian, ready to take me back into our fantasy world and keep me safe.

I jump when someone knocks on the door, listlessly slurp at a lump of ice cream as Aunt Vonda answers it. I know the sound of his voice, cringing as Aunt Vonda invites Miller inside.

My eyes won't lift. I just can't look at him. Not after I shattered his trust, too. Not with Ian hovering, waiting for me to choose him over a guy who might or might not be in a relationship with the biggest bitch I've ever met.

I know better than to blame Miller. He believed in me and I failed him, failed Aleah.

I'll never live this down.

His hand appears in my vision, taking the ice cream away from me. I look up then, see him turn away from Aunt Vonda and head for the door. After a deep sigh, a quick glance at the chair where Ian's phantom sits, I follow after Miller, if only for my sugary fix and to say goodbye.

It's more than either of those things driving me, but I refuse to listen to the part of me who wants him here.

The part of me who sends Ian away as I enter the stairwell and climb to the roof.

We end up perched on the edge of the community picnic table, the heat of the summer night melting the ice cream so fast it's a mess in short order. Miller takes the spoon from me, helps himself to a part that's still frozen before handing it back.

I can handle this silent sitting and eating, allowing the sugar to spark in my veins, his calm, quiet company keeping me from hurling the remains over the ledge in a fit of anger.

When he finally speaks, he's the angry one.

"I guess I shouldn't be surprised how petty and childish," for a moment my heart seizes until he finishes the sentence, "Bianca is being." My pain releases then and I shiver, despite the heat of the air.

I don't think I could bear it if Miller thought about me that way.

"It's her down to the ground," he goes on, the spoon making swirls in the remaining slush of the ice cream.

"Why are you dating her?" I lean forward, elbows on knees, head in my hands. It's none of my business. I have no right to ask.

Miller doesn't answer. I look up, see him scowling, brows drawn together.

"Who told you Bianca and I were seeing each other?" His voice is harsh, angry all over again.

I kick myself for believing a single word she's

said to me since we met.

"Bianca did." I look down again. His heavy sigh tells me I've been an idiot about this, too. So what else is new?

"I'm not even going to deny it," he says, voice chilly with anger. "Except to say she's a master manipulator, Riley. I'm only just beginning to see how well she's played me over the years."

"Okay then," I say, knowing I'm pushing him, but not caring. "Why are you friends, then? Because you are friends, aren't you?"

Miller's tension eases a little, physically settling from tight anger to reluctant acceptance. "The same reason we all are," he says. I can only see his hands, loose around the spoon and ice cream carton, resting in his lap. "She's a rising star. And we all want some of what she has."

I scowl at the ground. "That's a horrible reason to be anyone's friend."

Miller's grunt straightens me up as he sets the carton aside, hands running down his thighs. "You're right about that," he says, voice soft and eyes far away.

All at once I'm not really upset anymore. Just sad I blew it. Bianca might be a bitch, but this was my failure. So, the question then becomes am I going to let it stop me, or am I going to be the person who keeps going?

"I don't know if I can handle this," I say. "The ups and downs. I've cried more the last week than I have since Ian died." Okay, some of the tears were over Ian, so it's not fair, really.

Miller frowns, but doesn't ask questions. And I realize then I've told him nothing of who I was, the girl I left behind in Clifton.

It's a natural thing to share with him, then. About how Ian and I were best friends since kindergarten. How I was his only friend through much of his childhood because of the leukemia keeping him out of school. How tough it was for him when his remissions only lasted a few months at a time. When I finally asked him out in grade ten, he wanted to say no, because it wasn't fair to me.

The last two years with him, some days good, most of them bad, while he fought with the disease and tried to live his life as if he was healthy. The moment he passed into his last coma. The day he died.

"This is Ian's fault," I say at last. "He made me promise to chase my dream. He loved to watch me on stage. But, Miller, this is so different from what I know. What I did before, it was easy. I never had to audition, not really. It was one show to the next, because we had so few actors in town to draw from. There, I'm a big fish. Here, I'm barely a guppy." I hug myself. "And my mother, she wanted me to do this, too." I sink into the scary question rising from my confession. "So, is this what I really want, or am I doing it because of them? To piss off my dad?" I finally admit it. "It used to be fun. It's not anymore, not the real parts of it. The audition parts and the people I need to impress. Maybe I'm meant to be an amateur after all."

Miller doesn't say anything as I go on, processing my thoughts out loud, something I used to only do with Ian. The reality of it isn't lost on me as I forge on anyway.

"Ian was the star," I say. "Everyone loved him." I lean back, look at my hands in my lap, picture his in mine, how he would hold on no matter how much pain he was in, how weak he was, just wanting the connection. But my memory doesn't manifest a full version of Ian and, in a moment or so, my hands are alone. "Ian was so positive, no matter how sick he became. He said I was his star, and loved I found joy in acting." I feel a hiccup of a sob rising. "But my mother cheated on my father and now I know my dad lied to me about how she died. He's been an asshole to me my whole life because he's been trying to punish my mother. It's tainted my love for acting, too." *Why am I letting all of this out in front of him?* I'm making no sense, rambling on about things Miller hasn't a clue about, and yet I can't stop. "I don't want to be my mother." The woman who says she loves you and then runs off with someone else. Dies with that someone else so your father will hate you forever. "And I don't want to be Bianca." My gut clenches. "If that's where acting is taking me, I'm done right now."

I've run out of things to say, falling into confusion and the multiple broken hearts I've suffered in the last little while.

Miller seems to sense I'm finished because he finally takes my hand, thumb running over the back, resting in my lap as his long fingers curl around mine.

"The very fact you're worried," he says, "is your answer."

I look up, frowning. "Because I'm aware of it?"

He nods, smiles kindly, sadly. "I'm sorry about Ian," he says. "But he was right. You're meant to be on stage. Still, you can't do it for him or your mother." Miller looks away, but his hand remains in mine. "Thing is, girls like Bianca, they are like that from day one. Start out a bitch, you know?" He shrugs. "And as for your mother, why does her infidelity have to be about being wrong and not about her wanting to be happy?"

I chew my bottom lip. When I think about it that way, I feel the beginning of forgiveness for my mother.

"We all have the right to be happy," Miller says. "Even if it hurts the ones who love us. Because we're the only ones who matter, Rye."

I squeeze his hand. "I put Ian first for so long," I say, "I'm having a hard time believing that."

Miller tugs on my hand, turns me to face him. "I get it now," he says. "But it's time for Riley to decide if this is what she wants. To ignore the voices in her head and trust her instincts. Her heart."

My instincts want me to hug him. So I do. Miller holds me, cheek against my hair.

While I struggle to figure out if I even know who I am anymore.

# Chapter Twenty

Miller finally releases me. But he's not done.

"The first time I saw you," he says, eyes lighting up as the last of the sun fades behind him, "then later, that night in class. I knew you were a star in the making, Riley." His lips lift into a smile. "And when you performed, you blew me away. The street scene?" He lets out a rush of air, laughs, brows arching toward his hairline. "I've never been part of anything like it in my life. It's what every actor dreams of."

I'm trembling, remembering it, too. "It was awesome," I say. "But it was one moment."

He nods. "That's all life is," he says. "Moments strung together. And hopefully more of them are great than shitty." Miller sits back, resting his weight on his hands, looking out over the city. "I just think it would be a shame to quit before you know if you can find your voice more often than not." He meets my eyes, his gaze calm and steady. "Bianca may have been born a bitch, but you were born to act, Riley James."

I want to believe him. It's such a crappy moment to doubt myself while he gazes at me with such kindness.

"Hardship happens," he says. "Everyone has a story. But how we face what we've lived dictates our fate, if we let it."

I suddenly realize I have no idea what his story is. I've gushed all over him, dumped Ian and Mom and Dad on him and never once asked, though I've assumed. Rich kid, from New York, I've guessed. And though I know Bianca lied about everything else, I think about what she said about him having a breakdown, drug problem.

And I want to know more.

"How did you get into acting?" It seems a safer question than, "What's your hardship?" or "Are you still a drug addict?" Because I fear one will come across as a challenge and the other an accusation. As if I'm asking him what he could have possibly gone through that was harder than what I went through.

Miller surprises me with his shrug, the tilt of his head. And his words. "It's a long story," he says. "Parents died when I was six. Dumped in foster care." I stare, heart already hurting for him. "Got into trouble when I was thirteen, jacking stereos from cars, running drugs for local gangs." Now I'm gaping, surprised. He grins at me. "You don't have to look so shocked."

But I am. I really am. Only because now I'm thinking Bianca's little drug story might be true.

"Me and three others were tossed in a do-gooder program, dumped into a theater class with a bunch of rich kids." He sits forward again, stretches out his shoulders, graceful and nonchalant. "Bianca was one of them."

Now I'm really floored. "I take it you enjoyed yourself," I say.

His teeth flash in the fading light. "The best," he says.

Wait, I thought—

"But, you're rich," I blurt before I can censor myself.

Miller nods like me asking this way is no big deal. "I wasn't just drawn to acting," he says. "I loved everything about it. Wrote my first show at sixteen. Sold one at twenty." He grins. "And another. And another."

I ask him for names, and he rattles off three that make me tremble. One of them is a huge Broadway hit.

He's like, what. Twenty-four? And he's already a massive success.

And yet. I have to ask. "I know she's a liar," I say, "but Bianca said you..." How do I come out and say it? "You had a drug problem."

The hurt on his face makes me wince. I reach for his hand, squeezing it as he nods.

"That part of my life is over," he says. "Next time, ask her if she ever really knew me at all."

That sounds like a strange thing to do, but Miller is moving on and I'm not about to push him.

"I got tired," he says. "Stopped writing." His hands turn around themselves. "I wanted to act again, instead of being pressured to write." Miller grins at me. "Until I met you. You inspired me to tell stories again." That's the second time I've heard someone say I've been their inspiration in the last two days. It makes me blush. "I'm taking my time," he says. "But I'm loving writing again. Because of you."

I don't know what to say. He doesn't give me the chance to talk anyway.

"Here's my point," he says. "If I'd let my fears about pursuing my dreams to act stop me, I wouldn't have been doing something as benign as 'going home to Clifton.'" I shudder, nod. "I'd be in a gang, or strung out on drugs or dead. Instead, despite the hate from the rich kids, the fights I went through to break out of the life I was living, I kept going. And I'm alive, well, and on this rooftop tonight." He leans toward me. "With you."

I kiss his cheek on impulse, the rough stubble prickly on my skin.

"So I'm being a total idiot," I say.

Miller shakes his head. "No, Riley," he says. "You're being human. If this was supposed to be easy, more people would do it."

"Thank you for being honest," I say. "For sharing your story."

"You, too." He bumps my shoulder with his. "But the only person you should really be grateful to is you."

My heart swells open. I feel the draw of him. My need to kiss him, not just on the cheek, while my guilt over Ian fades. Now I know Bianca was never in the picture, my desire to be more than just friends returns with so much attraction behind it I feel myself flush.

Miller kisses my forehead as though he hasn't noticed, pulls my head down to his shoulder where I snuggle against his shirt, his collar against my cheek. "Riley," he says, his voice a little thick, "I wish I'd known about Ian. I would have done this all differently." I wonder what he means as he goes on. "But you need to know I'm falling in love with you."

Did he just really say—

I can only nod against his shoulder, breathing through my mouth to keep from crying, from blurting words I've only said to one other guy. Before I know if it's how I really feel.

"We'll go as slow as you want," Miller says, releasing me. "Just tell me if I'm off base and you want me to go."

My instincts are working perfectly as I lean

forward on impulse and press my lips to his. Miller kisses me in return, soft, the barest touch, fingers tracing down my cheek before I lean back.

"That's a 'we'll see?'" His eyes sparkle.

I'm smiling at last. "For all of it," I say.

Miller leaps from the picnic table, takes my hand and pulls me to my feet.

"I beg to differ." He's grinning suddenly, steering me toward the rooftop door.

"Sorry?" I try to turn, go back for the abandoned ice cream dish and spoon, but he's not allowing me to slow down or deviate from our path.

"You have an appointment," he says, glee in his words.

My stomach clenches all over again. "With who?"

Miller spins me around, jerking the door open and gesturing with a half bow for me to go first.

"Your director," he says. "In about," he glances at his watch, "twenty minutes, you have a new audition for another show."

# Chapter Twenty One

I'm walking down the stairs, still in shock at Miller's pronouncement, but unable to say a word about it. We're actually inside Aunt Vonda's apartment before I turn around and stare at him with what I know has to be deer vs. headlights terror.

"I can't," I say, even as my heart begs me to go.

Miller ignores my denial, all casual as he addresses Aunt Vonda instead of me. "Another audition," he says. "I was talking to a friend of a friend. Turns out the lead in a small production quit at the last minute and the director is desperate." He finally meets my eyes, his sparkling with humor. "And you are perfect for the role."

He gently turns me around, pushes me toward the back of the apartment. "Touch yourself up," he says, "and let's go."

I'm moving as though he's controlling me, slipping into my room, to the bathroom. He's right, I'm a mess from all the crying, a drip of ice cream clinging as embarrassing evidence to my chin. A quick splash of water and a puff of powder to take the bright pink from my cheeks and I'm finger-combing my curls out before tying them back in a loose ponytail I hope looks fashionably tousled instead of frantically clawed.

I pause at my desk, pull free a fresh headshot. *Am I really doing this?* I've lost my mind, clearly, and yet I giggle in mild hysteria at the thought of throwing caution to the wind as I exit my room and head out to Miller's grin and Aunt Vonda's bouncing happiness.

She hugs me carefully, kisses my cheek. Shakes me a little when we part. "This time," she says, "you make sure they know who Riley James is."

I nod, still unable to speak. Miller liberates the headshot from my sweating hand and laces his fingers through mine before leading me to the door.

And out into the hall. Down the elevator while I focus on breathing and not bursting into more anxious laughter.

It helps he's holding my hand. In fact, I never want him to stop.

As we cross the street heading in the opposite direction to my last audition, this time further into Hell's Kitchen, I promise myself one more try. That's it. *If I can't work my way through an audition without being a freak, without freezing up and crying all over the place, I have no right to pursue this dream.*

I'll just have to make sure my fear—and Bianca's stupid influence—don't overwhelm me this time.

I have a sudden burst of terror she's somehow found out about Miller's new plan as he leads me around a corner and to a small door on the side of a building, the entry painted solid black. I don't think I can go through with it if she's sitting in the audience again, laughing at me. Telling the director I'm no Marie St. Claire. Miller doesn't force me to talk, stays quiet, though he gallantly opens the door for me as he had on the roof and bows. He waits with quiet blue eyes for me to make up my mind.

It's his solid support, neither pushy nor judging, that makes my decision for me. I know, no matter what I decide—if I fail this time or not—Miller doesn't care. He just wants me to be happy doing what I love.

*I really am falling for him.*

My feet carry me through the door, my heels tapping on the hard floor as the light disappears behind me, the exit swinging shut with a solid thud. We're backstage in a tiny theater, so small we don't have far to go, squeezing down a narrow pass between the wings and the walls, to reach the side door and the main auditorium.

The sound of a muffled voice reaches me and makes this whole moment real. I almost balk.

Until I feel Miller's hand on my shoulder, a gentle squeeze telling me he's there. Not an apparition I've summoned from memory, nor a ghostly presence I can't bear to release out of fear of forgetting his love, of being alone. But real, alive, supporting me just by the touch of his fingers on my hair, sweeping it back from my neck.

My feet keep moving, my pulse settling with just that little piece of knowledge, something to cling to, to bolster my damaged confidence. *Miller is with me. He believes in me. And I can do this.*

I emerge from the black-painted back to the shabby little theater just as a young woman steps down from the stage. Hers was the voice I heard, now silenced in the quiet space. The director sits behind a small lap desk, reclining in one of the theater seats, a frown on her face. And she's not alone. But this time it's not Bianca whispering in the director's ear.

It's Aleah.

My friend spots me, waves, gestures for me to

come forward. Miller hands me back my headshot and resume, clean and unrumpled, a state I know it wouldn't have been in had I been the one to carry it all this way. I leave him, still in a daze, the coldness of my fingers and palm sharply acute at the loss of his touch.

We're the only people left in the theater and I realize Miller and Aleah must have pulled serious strings to allow me to audition without an appointment. The director, an attractive woman with super short blonde hair and a sparkling nose stud, raises an eyebrow at me as I approach.

She stands, offers her hand. I shake it. "Riley James," I say, the first words I've spoken since Miller's coup became reality.

"Dae O'Ryan," she says in a clear, deep voice. I like her already, from the vine tattoo encircling her wrist and climbing her forearm to the punk band t-shirt she wears like a second skin.

I hand Dae my resume. "Thank you for seeing me," I say, amazed how calm and together I sound. I just hope I'm not fooling myself thinking I sound calm and together. For all I know, I'm acting like a total lunatic.

Dae just shrugs, offers a little smile, green eyes flickering to Aleah. "You came highly recommended," she says. "And you have the look I'm aiming for. Let's see what you can do."

I nod to Aleah, unable to make myself smile wider past the small, professional lip curl gracing my mouth. Auto-pilot guides me up the short flight of stairs to the stage where I turn in slow motion and look out over the seats.

And freeze all over again. *God damn it, this can't be happening!* But fear grabs hold of me and tightens its grip, squeezing my chest until I can't breathe, forcing my knees to wobble slightly, my skin tingling with excess adrenaline, heart certain it will burst at any moment.

Ian appears in the seats, sad face dying, as I'm dying.

Dae's face goes through anticipation to confusion and into disgust. She turns to Aleah even as I suffocate in my own terror, Bianca's face layered over my friend's, laughing at me.

*Amateur*, her phantom whispers. *Small town*.

I curse my over-active and practiced imagination its ability to mock me where once it brought me only comfort. But there is no comfort in Ian's crumpled face, in his dying ghost. Nor in the horrible, poisonous smile Bianca wears in Aleah's place.

"I have two weeks to get this production up and running," Dae says, breaking my desperate anguish, my freezing terror. Anger rings clear in her voice. "And you bring me someone who can't even audition?"

No, this can't happen, not again. Not when Miller sits without judgment, his small smile going nowhere, kind eyes telling me I can do it though I think he's wrong. I've blown it.

I'm no actor.

*Go home, loser*, Bianca tells me. *You don't have what it takes*.

*Riley*, Ian whispers with his dying breath.

I choke on her hate and his loss and know I'm done.

Dae meets my eyes, hers flat and unfriendly. "Thanks for coming out," she says. "And for wasting my time."

Bianca laughs out loud, though I can see Aleah's distress beyond the mirage.

Ian sighs, disappears, dead again, his last breath a rattling reminder of everything I've lost.

Something inside me snaps.

# Chapter Twenty Two

"If you don't mind," I say, crisp and clear as my temper fires up, mouth moving before I can cram it shut. "I just needed a moment to get into character." The lie falls easily from my lips, gut taking over where my brain is failing me miserably. "I'm ready."

I'm not. But my frozen state is gone, the cracking of my shell shattered by my surge of anger. This is just a tiny stage. A no-name director. Just a person in front of me, not some monster or someone out to hurt me. Ian is dead, has been for a year now. He's not real. This is real.

As for Bianca... her smirking presence fades from Aleah's tense but hopeful face as I mentally give the bitch in my mind the finger.

The monologue I rehearsed comes easily as I reach for it, falls around me like a familiar dress, soft and luxurious. The character of Delores I've kept, enhanced, added life to until she takes over as easily as though I stepped aside to allow her to speak. The world flows around me, the very air hugging me, the three people watching feeding Delores's need for them to understand her, to hear her plight and weep for her as she weeps.

As I weep. My knees ache from my fall to the stage, though this is the first time I've taken the part so far. Delores has driven me to collapse. But it's appropriate, she's at her breaking point, as I'm at mine, and I coax her into ending her speech while I bow our head and let the teardrops of frustration, anger and fear fall to the black-painted stage.

I return to myself, climb to my feet. Look into Dae's eyes.

And see absolute shock in her face. She's leaning forward over the back of the next chair, arms hanging loose, gaze bright with her own tears. Aleah claps silently, all scrunched up as she quivers next to Dae. But it's Miller's reaction I'm anxious to gauge. The smile he gives me, the bow and salute, tells me I've done all right.

*Screw you, Bianca Sullivan. I can do this.*

I've done this.

As Dae sits back, mouth still hanging open, Aleah hauls off and punches her in the arm.

Dae barely reacts, turning to stare at Aleah.

"Didn't we tell you?" My friend wiggles her head back and forth, lips in a told-you-so smirk. "Our girl, she blew you away."

Dae shakes her head, looks back at me, starts to smile. Stops. "That was..."

Miller claps softly. "Riley, that was brilliant."

Dae nods this time. "Brilliant." She breathes the word. "I've never... you're fabulous." She draws a breath, tosses her pen and clipboard to the floor. "The part is yours if you want it."

Aleah squeals and grabs Dae, kisses her firmly on the cheek while Miller continues to grin at me. Even as I do my best to process what Dae just said.

The part. Is mine. If I want it.

"I want it," I manage to say through my stunned

disbelief and stirring buzz of excitement at war with each other over how I'm supposed to feel at this moment.

Would my new director think less of me if I jumped up and down and screamed at the top of my lungs?

Dae stands and exits the row of seats, Aleah beside her giving me thumbs up and okay circles while doing a little dance down the row. I hold still while I continue to wonder and Dae speaks. "I have to tell you, though," Dae says as she climbs to the stage to shake my hand, "if I was a better person, I wouldn't offer it to you."

Is she taking it back? My hand closes reflexively on hers.

"I want it," I repeat quietly, with more reserve on the outside than I feel on the inside.

*Please don't make me beg.*

Dae laughs. "You're way better than this little shit show," she says. "But there's no way I'm turning down your kind of talent."

"I disagree." Miller stands at the foot of the stairs, arms crossed over his chest, eyes still locked on me. "Riley needs somewhere to break in and this show is far enough under the radar she can get some real experience while growing her skills."

I got the part.

I think I'm going to scream after all. And then throw up.

"Besides," Aleah says, coming to my side to hook her arm through mine as I swallow, lips quivering around a grin I can no longer contain past my shock. "With someone like Riley, maybe the show will get a little recognition. If you can get a critic in here to see her."

Dae is nodding, smiling, eyes bright. "You're right," she says, sounding softly desperate. "This might be the break we all need." She pauses then, guarded look crossing her face. "You can commit?"

It takes me a moment for my empathy to reach past the bubbling vortex of my emotions. The moment I do, I feel myself calm. This is natural, the need to be there for others. To be here for her as I was for Ian. I remember now, her last actor left her in a lurch. "I can commit," I say, realizing I'm simply repeating what she's said for the last few times I've spoken. "Thank you, I'm in."

Dae squeals, very uncharacteristic from what I've seen of her so far, and does a tap-dance routine that ends in a quick spin before rubbing her hands together. "We have to get you off book as fast as possible," she says, her mind clearly still spinning, though her body isn't, as she turns away from me and walks to the edge of the stage. Returns with a little bound volume I quickly flip through. "Moira dominates the entire play, so you'll have to learn fast." She pauses again. "You can do that?"

I nod, though all I see when I rifle through the pages is the name Moira over and over and wonder what I'm getting myself into.

"It's just one act," Dae says as though to reassure me. I meet her eyes as I see her name on the cover and she blushes. "Mine," she says, shrugs. "But two weeks… you're sure?"

No way am I turning her down, not now. I look up, even as fresh terror—though heated through with excitement the fear barely makes a dent in my need to say yes—burns a hole through my stomach.

"I'm sure," I say. "When's the first rehearsal?"

Not tonight, apparently. I'm dragged from the tiny theater and down the street to a crowded and noisy bar. We manage to snag a table in the back corner, the wobbling of it stilled by two books of matches so it won't dump our drinks on the floor. Dae buys the first round and raises her glass as they are delivered by our frazzled waitress.

"To Riley," she says.

"To Riley." Miller and Aleah clink glasses while I smile and blush.

"Thank you," I say. "For everything." I look at Aleah. "For trusting me."

Her teeth flash white against her skin.

"I know the perfect critic," Dae says. "I just have to play him right to get him to attend."

Aleah bites her lower lip, glances at me. "You think that's a good idea?"

Do I need to be worried? Even Miller looks slightly nauseated.

"Darren Wright is a great guy," Dae says. Rolls her eyes. "Okay, so he pans more shows than he loves."

"He totally dissed Bianca in her last show," Aleah says. Reaches for my hand and squeezes it. "You're way better than her, so no comparison. Still."

I'm what? I almost choke on my wine.

"We need a better venue." Dae looks suddenly worried. "Maybe I need to do some other recasting, too."

"I love the theater," I say on impulse. "It's a great spot."

Dae beams at me. "Okay, then," she says. Breathes and gulps her beer. Sets it down with a clatter and laughs. "I haven't been this excited about a show in ages."

She leans toward me, pointing one finger wrapped in a wire ring, the three gemstones embedded in it sparkling in the overheads, drawing my eye, reminding me of the stage lights. "You pull this off," she says, "you do what you did tonight in front of an audience, and you, Riley James, will be a star."

# Chapter Twenty Three

It's after eleven when Miller and I leave Aleah and Dae at the bar. Dae is a little drunk by then, giggling into her beer glass while Aleah whispers in her ear. I glance over my shoulder, see them kissing and blush, but not because of their open affection, or the fact they are gay.

But because seeing them so intimate makes me think about Miller.

We reach the fresh air of the street and I stretch up onto my tiptoes, feeling myself expand outward as my happiness finally surges through me, releasing the last of my fear. As long as I keep telling myself it's a small theater, the people in the audience are just that—people—I know I'm going to be okay.

Miller turns me in a circle, dips me carefully while a few passing pedestrians applaud and laugh, our particular magic infecting them with smiles.

When he straightens up, I step away. "How can I ever thank you for not letting me quit?"

He shakes his head, hands in his pockets, smiling at me with a sexy little grin I want to kiss suddenly.

My stomach tingles, skin rushing with heat as he speaks.

"You did it," he says. "Like I knew you would."

I approach, poke him in the chest with one finger. "Maybe," I say. "Maybe not. Probably not."

Miller's blue eyes darken. "You would have," he says. "If you never met me. Because you wouldn't have met Bianca."

No way is she ruining this moment.

"It's worth it," I say. "Because I met you." And Aleah. And Piper.

Miller doesn't answer, though the clouds leave his face and he's smiling again.

I need to change the subject. If I don't, I'm going to pounce on him and kiss him right here on the street. Unfortunately, my mind is on the possibilities and my question comes out in a low tone, private, inviting. "I didn't know Aleah and Dae were a couple."

Because talking about couples is exactly where my head is right now. I feel like I'm drunk, though I'm completely in control of myself. Not my hormones, no. But of me, yes.

I really am kidding myself.

Miller's hand finds mine, sparking heat between us as we turn and begin our stroll home.

"They aren't," Miller says. "Or, they weren't. Aleah's been in love with Dae for over a year, but Dae just came out of a really horrible relationship and she's been focusing on her writing. They've both been playing cat and mouse for ages. So it's nice to see Dae finally opening up again." He sighs. "Aleah deserves to be happy. And so does Dae."

"And so does Miller?" I don't know why I frame it as a question.

He nods. "And so does Miller," he says, fingers tightening on mine.

We're at the corner where we can either turn

toward Aunt Vonda's or to his place. And I impulsively steer him toward his loft.

"I'm not ready for tonight to end yet," I say. "If that's okay?"

Miller squeezes my hand, blue eyes full of sweet tenderness and soft joy. "It's way more than okay," he says.

I'm surprised to find the loft is actually empty for once, just the two of us.

"Show tonight," Miller says. "Everyone will be back after midnight or so, probably." He goes to the kitchen, pulls open the fridge. Offers me a cooler. I wave him off, dumping my purse on the counter.

"I'm already drunk," I say, laughing.

He laughs with me, puts the cooler back, leans against the door. "You had one glass of wine."

"I'm drunk on happy," I say. This moment feels endless, all soft around the edges. I feel like my impulse control has been cut, my need to hold back from Miller severed by the absolute joy buzzing through my veins. I kick off my shoes as I cross to him. Hesitate only a moment before running my hands up his chest, starting at his stomach, feeling his abs tighten under my touch. "You know what it feels like, Miller?" I lean in to him, slipping one leg between his, resting my cheek on his shoulder as my hands descend again, sliding around his waist to his back, fingers hooking in the waistband of his jeans. "I thought I'd never find it again, this feeling."

I've only ever touched one other guy this way. Miller is an entirely different experience from Ian. Where my lost boyfriend was bony, his muscles soft from illness, Miller's chest is all ridges, firm skin over his ribcage, hard pecs flexing under my touch. Maybe I should be feeling guilty right now, but I'm far too deep into these new sensations to let myself go there.

Far too into Miller.

I hear him clear his throat, look up to see his nostrils flare, his cheeks pink, pupils dilated.

"I know exactly what you mean," he says. His hands rise, slip over my back, one coiling in my hair, tangling there. "But it gets better."

I can't imagine. I press closer, the tight, hard heat under his zipper pressing against my lower abdomen. It's been over a year since I had sex, since Ian was able and had the strength. I miss it, with a burning desire I used to wonder if I imagined those times we were able to sleep together.

My fingers act without my permission, though I would have granted them absolute freedom if I'd known their intent. His shirt-tail pulls free in a single tug, my hands under his clothes, stroking the smooth, warm skin of his lower back as he arches away from the fridge so my touch can roam.

He feels amazing. Alive and real, solid. Healthy. So strange not to encounter a shunt at his side, old scars from a tube to open a lung after it collapsed. Just smooth, hot skin quivering when I stroke it.

Miller watches me with his blue eyes, jaw clenching once as I lightly trace my nails down the full length of his back from his shoulders to his waist.

"Riley," he half whispers, half moans my name.

"Miller," I say. "How could the worst of nights turn into something so magical?" I know I should leave, that it's too soon. I really barely know him. And Ian... no. I won't think of Ian. Not with Miller so close to me, with his trembling hands holding me, the need in his eyes.

For me. And I need him, too. More than I've ever needed anyone.

He kisses me without warning, mouth

descending, lips parted. The instant he moves, I rise on my toes to meet him, one arm free of his shirt to wrap around his neck.

Miller's hands lift me, set me on the counter. My legs slide around his hips, my dress tangling as he brushes it firmly aside, hands sliding up my thighs as he breathes into me, mouth hot, breath hot, tongue dancing with mine as I fight to get closer to him.

I'm moaning soft, panting breaths when he pulls away. I jerk him back, forehead pressed to his.

"I don't want to ruin this," he says, anguish in his voice, panic in his beautiful blue eyes. "Riley..."

"You can't," I say, kissing his cheek, his temple, tongue exploring his ear as he leans into me again, hands climbing higher up my thighs, fingers sliding over the curve of skin. I wiggle so the hardness of him rubs against me, making me shiver, moan louder, my head tossing back before I can stop it. He's a craving I need to satisfy suddenly, my mind no longer my own. I will not run.

Miller's mouth closes on my throat, travels with haste down my neck to my shoulder as I slip one hand between us and cup him through his jeans. His hips thrust toward me, my fingers closing around him, my knuckles wet from my own moisture as they rub with his rhythm. Another moan, my free hand tightening on his back, nails digging into his skin through his shirt as Miller grinds himself against me.

My fingers fumble for his zipper, the button, jerk them aside. The thin band of his underwear hugs my hand as my fingers descend into curly hair and grasps the thick heat of soft flesh eagerly waiting for me. It's Miller's turn to groan, head down, forehead on my shoulder.

"Riley." He whispers my name before looking

up, meeting my eyes.

Lifts me from the counter and carries me to his bedroom door.

# Chapter Twenty Four

It slams shut behind us when my toes eagerly hook the edge and shove it closed. I'm laughing, breathless as he lays me on the bed, body hovering over me. I release him long enough to run my fingers through his hair, to stroke his cheeks in a sudden lull of passion. I just want to look at him, admire his beauty.

And then he kisses me and the lull surges into need so powerful I feel an animal rising inside me.

My feet hook his waistband and shove his jeans from his hips, catching the edge of his underwear with my right big toe. Miller wriggles, the tip of him eager and quivering as he shakes himself loose from the confining fabric. I stroke him softly once before he bends to nip at my ear.

Leaves me a moment. I'm panting, jerking off my underwear, pulling my dress over my head, just wanting him back with me. On top of me.

Inside me.

Miller brings a black square with him as he reappears. "You or me?"

I grab it from him, tear it savagely with my teeth. Slip the cool circle of latex from the packet and guide my hands down his stomach, eyes locked on his. My other hand braces against his chest. I want to watch his face, see his reaction. I love this part, did with Ian—

I won't think of Ian. Not while I'm slipping the condom over Miller's pulsing tip, the skin flaming hot, tight and already wet with his own moisture. Miller's lips quiver as I slide the silky latex down toward his thick base, my head rising, my tongue licking across the beads of moisture now standing on his lip.

My hand retreats from the heartbeat pulsing through his thick heat, grasps his hair when I slide my heels up the backs of his calves and pull him toward me. Lick his lip, bite the edge.

Miller leans in slowly, so slowly, teasing me as I've done him. Now it's my turn to quiver and anticipate as he braces himself on one hand, left one sliding between my thighs, tracing over my skin toward my passion, waiting, anticipating his touch with almost painful tension.

His thumb skims my clit, exposed and jumping, and I gasp his name. Miller's jaw grinds as he bends, still slowly, hips dropping, the head of him brushing across me. The slippery latex makes a smooth track over my wetness, clinging as it passes, sending shivers of need through my lower body. I can feel my climax rising before I even know what he feels like inside me, I'm so deep into him.

I can't stand it anymore, though I know when I grasp his firm ass in one hand neither of us will last very long once his straining, vibrating heat finds a home where it belongs. But it doesn't matter, not now. And he seems to agree as his body follows my lead.

He's still going easy, going slow. I'm done with slow. My hips lift, demanding, and when Miller slides inside me, his pelvis hitting mine in a single surge, he gasps into my hair and thrusts harder.

I'm floating, flying, better than any time on stage, better than the greatest dream I've ever had. He is perfect, his shape, his size, thrumming inside me to the pulse of his heart and the strength of his passion. I arch from the bed, pulling him closer, needing all of him with me, our lips chasing each other as the thudding beat of my own body burns and rises and races down to our connection, until the giant waves take over.

Crest.

Break across me in their pounding rhythm.

I don't want it to end, cling to him as he shudders on top of me, within me, feel the crashing surf turn to ripples and fade away again as Miller sinks to the bed, cheek against mine, panting breath in my ear.

He pulls back and kisses me, sweet and soft, before nuzzling my neck. "Riley James," he whispers. "You astonish me."

I kiss him, okay with slow now as my body sinks into contentment. Until he moves, slipping free, the condom's velvet surface sliding loose and I feel stirring. Know I'm far from done with him.

His mouth explores my neck another moment before he retreats to the bathroom. Returns to sink down next to me and cuddle me against his chest. My fingers drift down to stroke his now soft flesh, though I can feel him beginning to stiffen again at my touch and giggle, knowing I'm not the only one who isn't quite ready to call it a night.

Miller's teeth nibble my ear. "I don't know why," he says, "but I assumed you were a virgin."

I laugh, frowning through it. "Why?"

"When you talked about Ian," Miller says. "I assumed he wasn't strong enough."

I'm suddenly sad, nodding into his chest. Only

then do I accept this is totally different. "He wasn't always weak from the drugs," I say. "And I think if it had been up to him, we would have never slept together. He was so sweet, he didn't want me to regret anything about us after he died."

Miller nods into my hair, fingers stroking over my arm, tracing across my shoulder to the strap of my bra. I didn't even think to take it off.

Probably because he drove thinking away the moment he kissed me.

"I had to buy the condoms our first night," I say, smiling at the memory of Ian sitting in the front seat of the car, blushing and grinning. It makes me happy to think I can talk about Ian with Miller and not feel any guilt. "I think I shocked him, but he agreed to it. He was in remission at the time. We thought maybe it was a good sign." I swallow a little harder than I expected to. "It was really the only time we let ourselves believe he might be okay. But the cancer came back, just like always." That is very difficult to say, making my voice rough, my eyes burn, but I push on. "Over the few years or so we did have sex, I was mostly the aggressor." At this, I do feel a pang of guilt. "Sometimes he couldn't." I shook my head against Miller's chest. "But I loved him and I wanted him to know what it could be like for us, in case we could have a normal life together."

"In case he lived?" Miller's voice sounds sad.

I shrug. "We talked about it sometimes. What if's. But neither of us really believed he'd survive." Does that make me a bad person? Ian didn't seem to think so.

Miller's fingers slip my bra strap from my shoulder. "I'm sorry, Riley."

I shake my head, look up into his eyes. "I'm not," I say. "I had a great love early. So many people don't even get one. And I…"

Miller doesn't say anything, but his eyes are smiling. Hopeful.

And I force myself to speak even as my heart acknowledges what I've been trying to silence . "And I think I get two."

Miller crushes me to him suddenly, kissing me, rough and a little wild. I dive into it, welcome his desperation, drive my tongue into his mouth, my hands pulling at his hair to seal him against me.

We part, panting, the heat between my legs sending tingles from my hips to my toes. He must see it in my eyes and I know I see renewed passion in his.

I'm done being careful and cautious and guilty.

And then my phone vibrates. I jerk upright, stare at my purse.

"Damn it," I say, realizing what the alarm means.

Miller lets me go as I nab my bag and check my phone. I groan. Fall back beside him, the offending device between us.

"I have to go," I say. Show him the alarm. "I have to work at 7AM."

Miller laughs, strokes my hair back from my cheek. "So responsible," he says. But it's kind, warm and full of humor.

I toss the phone aside, hook my leg over his hip. "Who needs sleep?"

And kiss him.

Except now I can hear the front door open, the sound of voices, laughter, someone singing. The gang has arrived, or is beginning to. I find myself blushing even as Miller sighs and rolls his eyes.

"I promise," he says, leaning in to kiss my shoulder, "tomorrow night, I'll make sure we have the place to ourselves. All night." His eyebrows wiggle suggestively and I laugh.

Kiss his nose. His lips. So tempted to just say screw it.

Someone knocks on the door, but doesn't open it, thankfully. "Miller, where's the beer?"

Laughter.

"I have to go." I retrieve my underwear, slip them on as Miller stands, still naked, and hands me my dress. My eyes rove over him as I toss it over my head, wriggling into it as he watches with hungry eyes.

I grab my purse, dump in my phone while he pulls on his jeans, no underwear, follows me to the door. Kisses me deeply, arm around my waist, pushing me into the knob. I don't care, because I'm kissing him back.

I wait, heart fluttering as he jerks on a t-shirt, reaches for his fly. My fingers do the duty, tucking his hardening heat inside before I carefully do up the zipper and button the top, fingers lingering over the line of soft skin just below his waistband. Miller groans, kisses me again.

"You'd better go," he growls in my ear, "or you're not going anywhere."

So tempting. Until a familiar voice comes calling to the sound of another knock.

I pull the door open, grin at Piper who stares with huge eyes as Miller and I stroll out of his room. Piper's gaze settles into narrowed humor as he slaps Miller's ass.

"About time," he sniffs and walks away.

I don't meet anyone's eyes, now slightly embarrassed, though not by what I've just done. Only that everyone is watching and has to know we just slept together. Miller holds my hand all the way to the door. One twitch of my gaze falls on Piper sitting with Ruben. Then I'm looking at the elevator, eyes straight ahead, shoulders back while Miller laughs softly in my ear.

He kisses me as we wait for the door to open, follows me with his hands and his lips into the elevator. "I'm walking you home."

I shake my head, knowing I need to make a clean break if I'm going to say goodbye to him at all tonight. "I'll grab a cab."

Miller hesitates. Kisses me again. He really has to stop doing that.

"I love you." The doors grind, closing and he's forced to back away as the panel slides shut. I blow him a kiss, no time to tell him I think I love him too, because I'm already on the way down. I fall back against the far wall as the elevator sinks to the bottom floor, my heart soaring.

I bounce to the corner, hail a cab. Rejoice in the back seat all the way home, singing and laughing, my heart so full I feel like my life can't get any better.

I'm still humming when I pay the smiling cabby, when I climb the stairs to the front door of Aunt Vonda's building. All the way up to her floor and into the hall, unable to quell the tune escaping me and not wanting to anyway. My purse swings in my hand, my feet light and barely touching the floor. When I catch the sound of loud voices, my head comes up at last, clears me from the fog I've been in. I spot a neighbor peeking out before she slams her door in my face.

Aunt Vonda's is just ahead. A thin stream of light escapes through the partially opened entrance and I panic. I rush toward it, imagining the absolute worst.

Someone broke in.

She's been hurt, bleeding, dying even.

Waiting for me to come home and rescue her.

My phone is already out, 9-1-1 tapped in, thumb hovering over send, the raised voices growing in volume as I burst through and into the apartment. My purse rises in my free hand like a weapon. Ready to whack her attacker and make him wish he'd never been born.

I stop, stare, my heart crashing to the floor along with my bag as it slips from my numb fingers. My father spins away from where he stands, halting in mid-shout at Aunt Vonda to face me, fury written all over him.

"Riley James," he snarls. "You're coming with me."

# Chapter Twenty Five

I can't respond. What can I say? My denial rips through me in a physical rush, like a response to a blow. Dad starts toward me, only to have Aunt Vonda grab his arm, stop him.

"You leave her be," she says, angry and shaking. "You hear me Richard? You leave that girl alone."

Dad pulls free of her. "I'm doing nothing of the sort," he snaps. "I've had enough of this foolishness." He meets my eyes, his burning with rage. "Where the hell have you been?"

"Out." Is he serious? He can't be serious. This, this isn't real. I'm imagining it, digging up my worst nightmare possible. I just need to shut off my fantasy and he'll vanish.

Only he doesn't and my response just fuels his anger. I might as well have lit a match under Dad's last firework. "Don't you dare take that tone with me." His voice roars through the kitchen as my knees quiver and my stomach joins my heart at my feet. "I asked you a question."

"I was with Miller." I'm not thinking straight. I need to get out of here, away from his yelling, his old hate. He makes me nervous when he yells at me, though he's never hit me. I just despise it, how small and pathetic I feel. I lose me in his words and forget where I am, who I am.

"Who is Miller?" Dad advances another step, Aunt Vonda clinging to him again. I back up, scrambling on my heels, fear surging.

"My friend." *What is he looking for? Why is he here? I'm a grown woman, he can't control me. And yet, here he stands, thinking he can.* "I was cast in my first show tonight and we were celebrating." He has to be proud of me, but I know he's not. This is the worst possible news I could hand my dad.

He spins on Aunt Vonda, her pale face still furious to match his own rage. "You were supposed to be taking care of her," he's still yelling. I can only imagine the neighbors are calling the cops by now, "not letting her run around with losers like some theater tramp."

I gasp, free hand rising to my chest, the other weighed down with my phone still ready to dial emergency. It's just a slim piece of plastic and glass, but it feels like I'm holding up a ton of bricks. *Did my father just call me a —*

Vonda slaps Dad, so hard his head snaps to the side. She's not nearly his height and he looms over her with his fireman's bulk, but she doesn't look even a hint afraid of him as the sound of the blow rings in the suddenly silent kitchen.

"Don't you ever," she snarls at him. "Riley is not Marie."

I snapped earlier, on stage, out of the control Bianca held over me. This time when I feel myself crack open, it's to the sound of my mother's name.

"Liar!" I rush at him with my old fear burned away, anger flaring in its stead. I hit him myself, punch him in the chest as he turns toward me, dodge him when he tries to grab me. "You asshole. Mom didn't die from an illness. She died in an accident. She was leaving you, you fucking coward."

I see his own hand rise, Aunt Vonda grabbing for his arm even as I face him, jaw out, daring him to do it. "Hit me," I snarl in his face, "and you will never, ever see me again."

Like that's much of a threat. He doesn't give a shit about me anyway. And yet, as I speak, Dad's face drains of color, his hand dropping as he steps back from me, fear in his own eyes. But not of me. I think he finally scared himself.

"No wonder Mom wanted to leave you." I can't pull back. I'm on the attack now, hating him, all of the old bitterness fed by my new knowledge and the power to finally stand up to him this way. "You controlling bastard. You didn't want her to be happy. Just like you don't want me to be happy. Well guess what." I step away from him as his anger begins to return, though only a fraction of what I've just faced down. "I'm twenty-one, Dad. You have no say in my life. And you had no say in hers, either."

He stands with his shoulders hunched, his brow furrowed, hurt in his eyes. But he doesn't speak. Aunt Vonda turns to me, reaches for me, but I step away from her, backing toward the door as she starts to cry.

"Fuck you, Dad," I say. Turn and leave, slamming the door behind me.

The old me would have paused to sob. The new me is so furious I can barely contain it. And can think of only one person I want to be with right now.

I stomp my way back to Miller's, knowing it's stupid and dangerous. Walking alone at this time of night is the dumbest ass thing I can possibly do. But my purse and my money are both on the floor at Aunt Vonda's and I'm not going back. I must have my bitch face on firmly enough no one dares approach me because it's short order before I'm pounding on the key to the elevator and stomping inside.

I shiver for a moment, alone and still angry, as the elevator carries me to Miller. I need to let this out, know he'll help me do it. Maybe I just need to fuck him and release this energy before I can think rationally.

The loft door is open as usual, though most of the crew is asleep already. I catch Ruben sitting up, eyes watching me as I cross toward Miller's room. He looks like he wants to speak, but doesn't. I wave a little, forget about him. Whatever his problem with me, I couldn't care less.

I'm here to see Miller.

He's probably asleep, too. It's not really fair to dump this on him, I know that, but I have nowhere else to go and he loves me. I just need his arms around me so I can shake off the anger, the fight, my hurt and find new ways to be the new me.

My hand is on the knob when I hear voices on the other side of the door. I frown, though my fingers are already turning, easing the entry to his bedroom open. My eyes lift to the pair in the room, the faint light of the bedside lamp casting shadows over Miller's bare torso where he sits on the end of the bed.

But fully lighting Bianca's naked body.

I can't move, held frozen as I was in the audition. I watch as she bends and kisses him.

And Miller… kisses her back.

Before she even turns to look at me, I can see her smirk, hear her laughing in my head, knowing she's made a fool of me as much as he has. This is some sick game they've contrived to make me think I can be an actor. They must be planning some huge crash and burn, a tag team of soul slayers.

She's the first to meet my eyes, blue flashing with contempt. "Hello, Riley," she says. "Back to sleep with my boyfriend again?"

Her boyfriend.

Miller's head whips around as he gapes at me, standing abruptly, pushing her away.

"Riley!" My name is a cry of pain as he turns from Bianca. Her hands grab him, pull him back, she's laughing.

"It's all right, lover," she says. "You can drop the act." Winks at me. "Time for Riley to know the truth about us."

I finally break free, back away from the door, heart shattering into a million pieces. Miller turns and roars at Bianca before spinning back to me. "Riley, no!"

I hear him yelling at her, but not the words he's using, because suddenly he's my Dad and Bianca is my mother and I can't make my lungs work. I spin, staggering for the door, hand pounding on the elevator buttons as I hear him racing out of the bedroom, calling my name, Bianca saying something, Aleah, too, in a sleepy, anxious voice. But the doors are open and I fall through, hitting the close button so hard they slide shut on Miller's panicked face.

This time I do sob, hands over my wide-open mouth as I run from what I've just seen, with nowhere to go and my soul burned to ash as I crash out the door and stumble into the street.

# Chapter Twenty Six

I trip my way down into the underground, fingers fumbling for a token I keep tucked in my phone case for emergencies as I lunge through the turnstile and into the tunnel. The subway arrives, only a few of us boarding. I find a seat in the far end of the car, huddle with my cheek pressed against the window and allow my tears to leak endlessly from my eyes.

I now know why Ruben looked like he wanted to say something. Probably not to warn me. Maybe to call out to Bianca that the show was over. I trusted Miller, believed in him. But he was with her all along.

Didn't he say they knew each other since he was a teenager? Sure, he denied they were a couple, but wait, no. He didn't. Specifically said he wouldn't deny it. Just said she was a master manipulator.

He. Never. Denied. It.

They had to have been together since they were young. How many other stupid girls had they played this game with? And was Aleah in on it? She had to be.

My friends were all liars. Just like my father.

That hurt, hurt a lot. Though as the long night on the subway passed into early morning, the first commuters ignoring me as they went about their busy days, my mind began to doubt. Maybe I misunderstood the situation?

*But Bianca was naked.*

No, wait. Maybe she was seducing him and he didn't want her to.

*But he was sitting there, hands on her waist, in his underwear. In his room. Where we just made love.*

I couldn't reconcile the fact he didn't seem to mind she was there. Or that when she bent toward him, his lips met hers.

Every scenario I pictured led back to exactly what Bianca said. That he was hers and they'd played me.

Whispers of doubt still rippled. After all, she'd done her best to ruin me so far. Surely she wouldn't hesitate to stoop to this, to some deception.

*But they were together. And he was holding her waist with his hands. Her naked waist while she smiled down at him.*

*And he kissed her.*

So much for love. Though I now cling to Ian's memory tighter than ever as I finally stand and make my way to the stop, get off ten blocks from Aunt Vonda's. But when I try to call up my dead love's shadow to walk beside me, I find myself alone.

He's gone and I can't seem to bring him back.

I need to walk then, to gulp fresh air and convince myself I'll always have Ian, no matter my present struggle with my imagination. I'll go back to the apartment. Climb into bed with my laptop and watch movies of us together until he returns. Until it's easy to roll on my side and imagine I feel him tucking in behind me.

When I emerge onto the street, the first thing I see is a marquis for a small theater. Bianca's theater, her name written there.

And my soul shrivels the rest of the way to nothing.

*I can't do this. I was wrong. They were just trying to hurt me.* Dae had to be in on it, too, lied to me... but, no. She was genuinely excited. So maybe I can act.

I stop on the street, anger appearing at last. I won't let this ruin me. I may not be tough enough to keep my tears inside, but wanting to act, trusting my talent, can be enough.

*Please, just let it be enough.*

My phone vibrates. I check it, see Miller has texted me at least twenty times, called me a dozen. I shut the thing off, clench my hand around it. He's just going to explain this away, start the charade up again. And I'll let him, I know I will, if I allow myself to listen.

*I still love him.*

I can't let this happen.

Aunt Vonda is behind the counter when I arrive at work, still in the clothes I wore last night. She hugs me, crying in front of customers and I pat her back, soothe her as best I can. She chases her customers out, turns the closed sign before dragging me into the back and sitting me down.

I tell her what happened with Miller, sobbing again all over myself as she hands me a seemingly endless glob of fresh tissues, taking the old, snotty, soaking ones from me until my shoulders only heave occasionally and my hiccupping has dwindled. Aunt Vonda retrieves the last of the crumpled mess from me and dumps it in the overflowing trash.

"Miller called," she says, voice sad and low. "He told me what really happened."

I shake my head. "He told you what he wants

you to know." My heart has hardened against him, against Aleah, Piper. Bianca. "I'm an idiot."

Someone knocks on the door of the shop. Aunt Vonda tsks in frustration, looks out over my shoulder. Pales and smiles sadly at me.

"You can be an idiot in person," she says. "He's here."

I'm already trembling. "What? Can't you just send him away? I don't want to see him."

Aunt Vonda hesitates, then shakes her head. "I'll do no such thing," she says. Bends and kisses my forehead. "You have to face this, pet." She isn't taking no for an answer, I can tell. I know she's right. This is the new me. The strong me.

I drag myself to the door. Open the lock, switch the sign. Miller walks in.

He opens his mouth. I don't even think. I slap him across the face.

I can't help but draw a parallel between Dad last night and this act of violence toward Miller. But I've struck him before I can stop myself.

"I saw you kiss her," I say, voice calmer than I expect. "So don't bother, Miller. Just don't lie to me anymore."

His hurt and shock turn to his own anger. "You're going to believe Bianca," he says. "The last person you should trust."

I glare at him, temper flaring. "I know what I saw. Maybe she's the only one who hasn't been lying to me all along."

"If you really believe that," he backs away, cheek red from my hand, "I think I made a huge mistake."

"Did you ever." Trembling and furious, I spin around and march into the back.

Where I cry for a little while longer.

Aunt Vonda sends me home. I shower and change, collapsing on my bed. Toss fitfully in and out of sleep, nightmares of Bianca laughing at me jerking me awake. I can't even bring myself to retreat in search of Ian. I feel like I've totally sullied our memories by giving to Miller what I only ever gave to Ian.

My body. My heart.

It takes everything I have to muster the power to go to rehearsal. But I need to go, I've committed to the show. At least I have this one joy left to me if Miller is gone.

But as I enter the theater, see Dae speaking with some other actors, I feel my stomach sink. My fear of emptiness—not the good kind, but the flavor of emptiness sucking at my soul instead of making it grow—expands as I enter. Dae greets me with enthusiasm. I try to smile, dump my purse and carry my script to the stage. I think she can tell something is wrong, her excitement fading as I try so hard to shake off the hurt of last night and focus.

I open my mouth. And trash comes out. Garbage, crass and worthless. Acting, not feeling, not a hint or a breath of my private joy present. It's been crushed, destroyed with my heart. And I can only go through the motions while Dae scowls at me and I stumble through the words like an amateur.

Like the loser small town Bianca says I am.

Dae finally claps her hands, jerks my derailing train to an abrupt stop as I inwardly sob and rage at the unfairness of this. How I've allowed Miller and Bianca to take from me the last thing I love.

"What the hell?" Dae stomps onto the stage, her anger crystal clear. "We have two weeks. I expect your best every time we rehearse."

I stare at her, mute. Not sure how to tell her I'm a failure after all.

I spot Aleah over her shoulder, coming through the stage door and do the only thing I can. I bolt, running to my purse, hating I'm a coward, unable to stop myself as Aleah calls my name, Dae raging behind me in wordless fury.

I stop on the street. Bow my head. And sigh out my sharp, painful disappointment.

"You win," I whisper to Bianca's smirk, hovering in my mind. "I quit."

Ian finally returns to me, though his dying face, his hunched body at the corner as I pass, isn't helping me any.

Aunt Vonda is home when I arrive, following me to my bedroom when I retreat there without a word.

"You're back early," she says, worry in her voice as I reach into my closet and haul out the first suitcase. She cries out, rushes to me, but I shake her off gently and start packing.

"Pet," she says. "You can't just leave."

I don't answer her. Ignoring her pleas as she continues to try to talk me down. Her words are a jumbled mumble. I can't make them out through the buzzing in my head, the endless flow of Bianca's laughter.

It doesn't take me long to pack, the two suitcases, laptop bag and backpack all achingly familiar. Didn't I just arrive? And now I'm leaving again. I turn to Aunt Vonda who's fallen mute at the door, tears trickling down her face.

"Thank you for everything." I can't bring myself to hug her as I lug the two heavy bags out the door by their handles, loaded down in a train of possessions and failure. "I'm going home."

Not to Dad. Never again. But Susan and Dwight, I know they will give me a place to stay, until I can figure out college. I've never wanted to do the student loan thing, but I guess I don't have a choice now.

I won't put myself in a position to owe Dad anything.

"What about the show?" Aunt Vonda's voice is still full of tears.

That makes me pause, regret so pointed it jabs me in what remains of my heart. I feel like crying again, though I'm certain I have no tears left at all.

"I'm going to save up for college," I say. "Be a good girl. And forget any of this happened." Forget I let Bianca have her way. Allowed Miller to dirty my memories of Ian. My dream is as dead as my lost love and it's time I chose to be practical.

*I hate Dad is right. I hate it so much.*

The elevator dumps me in the parking garage and it takes me a few grunting minutes to lug my stuff out into the cool air of the underground. My hands are full, maneuvering the two big bags on wheels behind me, shoulders aching from the weight of my purse, laptop and backpack as I roll toward my parking space.

The van is gone, probably still at the shop, out back. Leaving me a full view of my car.

Jacked up on bricks. Tires and rims gone. Front window smashed. I slow as I near it, realize I'm not going anywhere, at least in my car. I see my stereo is missing when I drag my now overwhelmed and defeated ass to the driver's door. The thieves even pried open the glove box and slashed the seats as an extra insult to the assault.

One of my suitcases thuds to the ground as I release the handles and let my bags fall to the concrete. I can't cry, just shake my head, shoulders slumping. *My life just can't get shittier.*

I need to be careful what I wish for.

The desire to sink to the dirty garage floor and sob my heart out is a distant feeling. Instead, I turn and lift my bags again, hooking the large suitcase that fell over with my free hand and dragging it upright.

Head for the ramp to the outside on foot. To hail

a cab.
Exit Riley James.
Stage left.

# Chapter Twenty Seven

I sit at the bus station, hating the Port Authority terminal is only one block from Time's Square, three from Broadway, just another reminder of my failure. I hug my purse to me as a pair of young men argue together a row of seats down, one finally handing over some dirty bills, the other quick with a small plastic baggie. The security guard ignores them as though drug deals in the open are commonplace.

I guess they are. And it's really for the best I'm leaving.

I spent the entire drive over here in the back of the stinking cab telling myself that very thing. *It's best I'm leaving. Look at the prostitutes standing on the corners, their brittle smiles masking their hurt. It's best I'm leaving. The bums and the druggies who beg for change before following people into alleys to rob them at knife point.*

*It's best I'm leaving.*

I can't handle it here, I know that now. And though Clifton calls me, I know I won't stay there long, either. I don't belong there anymore. I'll find a job doing whatever I can, apply for state college and move on as soon as possible. Get a real job, a real career and forget any of this happened.

Forget I wasted my dream on a guy who didn't deserve me and a vindictive bitch who will probably end up a star.

Numbness has taken over from my anger and pain, forcing me into logic to save me from the ache I can barely stand when it surfaces from time to time. My bus ticket sticks to my sweaty fingers, the air conditioning either broken or nonexistent in this place of transition. *Are they like me, the people waiting for their bus, walking through past the shops like this isn't a hub to nowhere special? Normal, ordinary people, or broken, like me? Looking for a new chance when this one failed them?* I have a sudden image of me sitting in endless bus depots waiting for my next chance, my new start, only to fail over and over again.

She sits beside me, the spicy scent my first indication I know the intruder in my space. I glance over, not meeting her eyes, finding Aleah with her legs gracefully crossed, hands in her lap. She isn't looking at me, staring out the big, dirty windows at the city going on outside without me. I shift, uncomfortable, not sure what to say.

Did she know about Miller and Bianca?

"He's known her forever." Aleah's voice startles me, low but clear, conversational. "Since they were kids."

I nod, I've heard this from him already, but I want to close my ears because she's going to make excuses for Miller and I don't want to hear them.

But she goes on and the numb can't tune her out the way I'd like it to.

"He's been in love with her at least as long." She shakes her head, her full, wiry hair corkscrewing around her in a crown of shining curls. "Damned fool. I tried to tell him she wasn't worth his time. But I met him long after she did and I was way too late to talk him out of her."

She just verified what my damaged heart figured out last night, seeing him hold her naked body and kiss her. *Is that why Aleah's here? To tell me I'm right?*

Now I really want her to shut up, because this is only making me feel worse.

"That first show he wrote?" Aleah shifts in her seat. "He wrote it for Bianca. He wrote them all for her. And when he told her, do you know what she did?"

*I don't care. I don't care. I don't care.*

"She laughed in his face." Aleah sighs, an exhale of frustration even as my heart contracts for Miller despite hating him right now. *Okay, so he's her toy, I get that. He has no spine of his own, she's using him. It's not the strangest thing that's happened. Guys do stupid ass stuff for girls they love all the time.*

"When he sold the first one, Bianca, she came running." Aleah snorts a cynical laugh. "But no one would cast a nobody, even though Miller tried to influence the producers."

I almost smile, nasty and hurtful. *I hope they crushed her like she crushed me.*

"She rejected him when they wouldn't," Aleah said. "Led him on until he was a puppy dog in love and then snapped the leash so hard she almost killed him." I hear the fury in her voice, feel it in her body as she vibrates next to me. "I was the one who held his hand through the meltdown, made sure he didn't overdo the meds his shrink prescribed." *Meds. Bianca's drug problem? Real, too, then. Though not the kind of drugs I thought she meant.* "He wrote another play, for her. By then, I knew him well enough I wanted to beat the crap out of him for being such a blind ass." *That makes two of us.* "But he was in love, in hard and deep and she pulled him back in when she found out about the show."

I refuse to feel sorry for him even as I relent slightly. I know how hard love can hit. Losing Ian felt like part of me died. *Okay, so maybe I can forgive him. Eventually.*

"He sold that show, too," Aleah said. "And for the second time, when the producer said no to Bianca, she ripped Miller's heart out and handed it to him." She thumps her fists against her thighs. "I held his hand one more time, while he cried. I brought him out of the dark, took the damned drugs away, made him face the truth. Made him quit her. But he couldn't, Rye. He just couldn't let her go. And so he wrote a third show. Told the director and producer he wouldn't sell it unless they cast Bianca."

I turn to look at Aleah. She still scowls out the glass, not focused on me at all.

"They said they would. Took the show from him. And cut Bianca loose."

My heart screams it wasn't his fault, my hands closing convulsively knowing what Bianca would have done to him. To punish him.

"She broke Miller," Aleah says. "Shattered him into a million pieces. And he hasn't written another show since." She finally turns to meet my gaze. "He didn't go back to that damned shrink, either. He pulled himself back from the brink all on his own. Promised me—swore to me—he was done with her and her shit. But no matter what I do, what anyone does, he won't cut her loose completely. And the others, they love her because she's rising, going to be a star, don't you know." Aleah snorts. Takes a moment to let that sink in. "Except, things changed not so long ago."

This is the part I don't want to hear, and yet I cling to her words like a lifeline.

"He started writing again. After he met a young actor who blew us all away."

No, bad enough I've lost my love for the stage, but to think they hadn't lied to me. That I really was good... no, I can't tolerate it. Better to believe I was never anything. Could never be more than small town.

"He started smiling again," Aleah says. "Talking about acting instead of watching all of us play at it." She flops a hand over in her lap, silver rings sparkling. "He even welcomed her into our group, when no one else has been allowed to join us forever."

I stare, swallow bitterness and dead hope.

"He kissed her," I say. It's all I manage.

Aleah rolls her eyes, slaps my hand. "The only reason that bitch," her expressive voice drops to a hissing growl, "showed up to seduce our boy was to hurt you. She's already destroyed him enough to know how to do it again. But."

I cough softly around the choking sensation seizing my throat.

"But this time, he didn't break." Aleah's full lips lift into a small smile. "He lost it. You missed the whole thing, rabbiting like that." As though running away wasn't an option I should have considered. "I've never seen him so angry. Or stand up to Bianca like that. He frog-marched her down the stairs in her buck and dumped her ass on the street."

Now I'm wide-eyed and open mouthed. "He what?"

Aleah chuckles, crosses her arms over her chest, her sandaled foot bobbing over her crossed knee. "If Ruben hadn't moved his traitor ass, she'd have been in serious trouble. Last I saw he was covering her with his shirt and hailing a cab while she screamed at Miller like some kind of banshee from hell."

Classy. And I really, really wish I'd been there to

see it. I laugh out loud, sober. Then hang my head.

Aleah lets the silence go on a moment before speaking again. "He's a fool," she says. "And he's made so many mistakes with that bitch. But Riley, he's my closest friend. And I love him. Enough I'm here, with someone I thought was my other closest friend."

I twitch, reach out and take her hand, broken heart now sobbing silently for the mess I've made. For believing Bianca's carefully constructed half-truths.

"You've both screwed this solid," Aleah says. "But the saddest part isn't you leaving, Riley Skyley." I'll miss her nickname for me because I'm still going. Now out of humiliation and shame for how I treated Miller. "He's no angel, he admitted he kissed her. Lost his head when he saw the woman he always wanted, offering herself to him." Aleah lets me go, turns in her seat. "For that alone, I'd kick his ass so hard he'd never come down from it."

I nod, sniffle.

"Nope, the saddest part is Bianca is getting exactly what she wants." Aleah stands abruptly. "And I really worry that without you, I don't know if Miller will ever write again."

She leaves without another word, striding off, singing a wordless song to herself. Down the aisle, out the glass door and into the city, disappearing from my view.

From my life.

I shake in my seat, hating myself now as much as Bianca. Still mad at Miller for being a jerk. But knowing I chose to let her win.

Fucking Bianca.

I can't just let her win.

And yet. She's right about me. I blew it. I ran instead of standing my ground. Again. It seems

I've been running from one thing or to another since I arrived in New York. And now, here I am, everything a mess, and I'm about to leave.

I'm so confused, the ticket in my hands trembling as I stare at it.

And think of Ian.

Look up to see him standing there. Smiling in a beam of sunshine. Waving at me.

*Sweetie. I don't know what to do.* I lower my head so no one will see me cry, just in case. Because my heart is wide open, my soul begging for an answer from the shadowy image of my make-believe need. *If I'm supposed to stay, if this is where I'm supposed to be, I have to know. I have to find some kind of sign I can make this work. That I haven't ruined everything.*

I used to talk to Ian in my head all the time. Now it feels odd, as though he's not a part of me anymore. I'm a little light headed, and I have to open my mouth to draw a full breath of air.

Wait for a sign that's not coming. And my bus for home.

Someone walks past me, pauses. I wish they would just move on. But whoever it is bends, lifts something from the floor. Hesitates again.

"Miss?"

I look up at a young man, clean cut, lips curving a little. He's holding a piece of paper in his hand.

No, not paper. A photo. One of my headshots.

"You're beautiful," he says, before handing the sheet to me and moving on.

I sit there, dazed and shocked. Look down at myself smiling back.

There's no way this could have fallen out of my bag. And yet, there it is, there I am.

My eyes lift to the sunbeam, empty, though I can feel him with me again.

"Thank you," I whisper to Ian.

I have my answer.

The ticket goes in the trash as I man-handle my bags out the door.

# Chapter Twenty Eight

I hear Dae shouting from the lobby, push through the thin curtain to the auditorium and march my way to the stage. The girl she's screaming at is in tears, hand over her mouth as Dae dumps all over her.

Three steps up and I'm beside the girl, guiding her away from Dae who glares at me with wide eyes before opening her mouth to shout at me, too.

I'm done with people shouting at me. I hold up my script as calmly as I can and flip it open. "What's the scene?"

My presence, my collected composure, seems to floor her. She splutters and chokes as the cast stares at us. I still hear the girl sobbing quietly behind me, but I ignore her. I have to play this right or I'm out and I know it.

Dae finally pulls herself together, fury snapping on her face. "You're done," she says, hooking her thumb toward the door.

"I'm not," I challenge her, knowing pushing Dae will get me nowhere if I don't produce. My only remaining fear is I can't. That this is all for nothing and I've thrown my life into more chaos. But I feel fresh, alive again, my bags back at Aunt Vonda's, cheek still feeling her multiple kisses and neck tight from hugs, feet sore from tromping down the street in a hurry. I kick off my sandals, pick a page at random.

I've read the script over, at least parts of it, desperately reviewing it in the cab on the way over. So I'm aware of the story, and I'm able to sink partially into the part, grasping for Moira.

Who rises to the surface and takes over. I like her. She's sultry, full of spunk. She gives me an edge I lack in my own life, a harshness I embrace fully.

One of the guys responds as I give the first line, Moira pushing him. I feel him respond, fall into the role, the sexy and suggestive character putting a swing in my step, a thrust to my hip.

He stumbles over his line, breaking the moment. But it's enough. It has to be.

I turn, see Dae watching me with hope and fear and anger.

"You walked out on me once," she says. I catch sight of Aleah in one of the seats, watching, beaming. Blowing me kisses. And I smile at Dae.

"My evil twin was an idiot and a quitter," I say. "But that girl left on a bus for home." I hold out the script. "I'm here now and, if you'll have me, I'm going to give Moira the most authentic voice she's ever had."

Dae is still hesitant. I can see it on her face. And I can hardly blame her.

I cross to her, still holding the script between us like a peace offering.

"I'm sorry," I say. "All I can do is tell you it won't happen again. I know I'm not the only one who has issues. Or reasons not to trust."

Dae shrugs as though heaving a weight from her shoulders. "You quit on me again," she says, voice low and harsh, "and I'll ruin you."

"I quit on you again," I say, "and I'll already be ruined."

She nods. "Fine," she says. "Now, if you don't mind, we have less than two weeks," the rest of the cast groans softly, "and a hell of a lot to do if we're not going to bomb."

My chest loosens, knots unfurling from my stomach as I spin toward the others. "Hi," I say, "I'm Riley."

Enter an actor. Stage right.

I didn't think two weeks could pass so quickly. One minute I'm barely learning my lines and the next I'm preparing for opening night.

Bless Aunt Vonda. She embraced this flip over with gusto and enthusiasm. I will never be able to thank her enough for all the time off she gave me from the flower shop, the early mornings drilling me on my lines, the way she took care of me, not asking for anything in return.

I'm going to have to find some way to repay her.

Even better, I've spent the last thirteen days immersed in theater, in rehearsals on the tiny stage during the day, in a small, cramped space above it at night while a burlesque show does its best to draw a crowd. The place is old and rickety and the lights don't always work, but I don't care.

I'm an actor.

Aleah chose to come on board as crew, clamping herself to my hip from the moment I stepped off the stage that first night. Inseparable, my best friend. And I can only hug her and thank her repeatedly while she laughs at me.

I choose to ignore her suggestions I call Miller. Not to hurt her, or him, for that matter. I'm already moving past the night of darkness, as I think of it, letting go of how I feel about the way Bianca almost broke me. I know now I need to focus. To do this, on my own, without him. Without anyone. Just me. So I know I can.

So I can finally see him knowing I did it. That I only need me so I won't wonder if the reason I'm here is because he believes in me.

Silly, maybe. This need I have to succeed before I tell him I'm sorry. Like it will make me more powerful or on more solid, even ground. But I need to finish what I started before I can decide if being with Miller is something that will fit into my life.

As an actor.

I do see Piper, hold his hand when he tells me he's broken up with Ruben.

"That queen," he snarls before crying on my shoulder. "I should have known he was Bianca's bitch all along."

It's hard to see Piper suffer. But it's time we both got over it.

I walk to the theater tonight, down the humid streets, feeling the city around me, embracing it despite the honking horns and shouting, the rude pedestrians and angry bums. This is my city, now. And no one is going to take it away from me.

Especially not myself.

I pause at the marquis, smile up at my name in the buzzing, flickering lights even as they shut off a moment before flashing on again. I laugh. *How perfect.*

This place may be a little tattered and run down, not quite ready for the show. But it's been home for two weeks. And I can't think of a more fitting place for Riley James to show the world what she's made of.

Aunt Vonda hugged me on the way out of the apartment, already dressing to come to opening night herself.

"I love you, pet," she said, calling down the hall after me. "I'm so proud of you. Good luck tonight."

I smile at the marquis. *Thanks, Aunt Vonda. But I don't need luck.*

I'm going to be just fine.

The side door is open, welcomes me into the cool darkness. Feels like the air conditioning might be having trouble. Doesn't faze me in the slightest.

I don't think anything can tonight.

My dressing room—a tiny closet in the back of the theater—overflows with flowers. I laugh at Aunt Vonda, finding a bouquet from Aleah and Piper. I sniff the gorgeous roses and thank them silently for this traditional tribute.

"Riley." Malik hugs me, my leading man bubbling with excitement. So fun to work with Latanya's boyfriend, with someone I already knew and thought of as a friend before we worked together. He bounces back, dark eyes sparkling. "Oh my God, I'm so nervous. Are you nervous?" He fans himself before straightening his broad shoulders, voice dropping into a sexy bass. "My darling Moira," he says.

I swat at his chest, loving how close I've become with the cast. Two of the girls hurry by, waving and blowing me kisses as I grin at them and then up at Malik. Swoon back in an over-done version of my character.

"Alas," I say, "I never loved you, Raoul."

Dae happens to be striding by with her clipboard in her hand and groans.

"Tell me you're going to do a better job than that tonight," she snaps.

I laugh and lunge for her, kissing her cheek after a firm hug. She snorts and whacks me with her clipboard.

I'm high, floating all over again. Only this time,

as Malik leaves, head down, talking with Dae, I feel in balance with it. Like it's not controlling me, but I'm the one holding the reins. I'm not going to float away. I'm grounded, Moira firm inside me, ready to come out.

I've been holding back on purpose. Worried I'd use up the best parts of her in rehearsal. But as I look at myself in the mirror, I smile. Tonight is the night I let her out.

And then, we'll see. The critics, the haters, let them come.

Somehow, I know their attitudes and attempts to hold me back will never bother me again.

Aleah rushes to my door, knocks. "Half hour call," she says. "Ready?"

I kiss her cheek. "So ready," I say.

She grabs me, squeezes me, black t-shirt blending into the darkness of backstage, her eyes and teeth bright against her skin as she steps away, gaze sparkling. "I'm so proud of you," she says.

"I wouldn't be here without you," I say. "I love you, Aleah."

One of her hands covers her mouth before she bobs a nod. Lunges for me again and hugs me so hard I hear my ribs creak.

"Love you, too," she whispers hoarsely in my ear before hurrying away.

I sit in my dressing room, applying my makeup, hearing the others chattering as they pass my door. The crew, the cast, even Dae. They all sound nervous. And though I know I should be terrified, I can't summon any fear.

*Is that wrong? Do I need the fear to make this work?* But no, the giddy happiness, the joy I feel, is more than enough.

As I slowly transform physically into Moira, I whisper my lines to myself, sitting back at last to observe the large-eyed, red-lipped woman in the mirror, her hair in a French roll, sparkling fake diamonds in her ears. Old class gone to seed is my Moira.

I can't wait to get out there and share her with the world.

Then I can freak out when this is over.

Five minutes is called just as I adjust my clothes, the cross-tied dress skimming my body close. Heels follow, pumps just high enough I won't trip. I turn and leave my dressing room, almost running into Aleah as she hurries by. Grins at me as I sneak to the edge of the curtain and peek out when Malik vacates the post.

It's my first shock of reality. The small theater is full, thirty or so people waiting and watching, murmuring over the programs in their hands, faces I don't know. Faces I do. I spot Aunt Vonda in the front, nervously twisting her program in her hand while Susan and Dwight chat with her. So nice to see them here.

My biggest shock comes when I see Dad, two rows back from them. He's wearing a tie and a suit and I almost don't recognize him, eyes skimming over him before returning with a gasp of breath.

What is he doing here? My first flutter of nerves wakes, quashed by my sense of Moira. She won't let him ruin this, if that's his goal. He can just sit there and watch us. And weep for our talent.

I actually laugh at Moira and accept. Besides, I don't have time to let my anger seethe, because my eyes leave him and settle on the blonde on the other side of the aisle. Bianca sits with Ruben. He's whispering to her while she waves at him like an irritating fly.

My stomach settles instantly, the last thing I expect. But I smile and step away from the curtain's edge, thanking Bianca, Moira coiling like a snake, ready to strike her enemy dead with her performance. Seeing Dad shook me, but knowing Bianca is here...

I'm going to put on the show of my life just to show her what a real actor looks like.

She might be here to shake me, but she's given me a gift and I hope she chokes on it.

Aleah comes up behind me, pulling me back away from the stage as the lights flicker and go out on the other side of the curtain. She gives me a gentle shove through the edge and I'm on the stage, first position.

The lights go up, blinding in my eyes.

I call on Moira, embrace her eagerness and let myself go.

# Chapter Twenty Nine

I don't know how it's happened, but I'm bowing suddenly, hands grasped firmly in those of Malik and my stage daughter, Amber. They're smiling to the sound of applause, to the audience standing and clapping for us while the lights still blind me.

I release their hands, blow Aunt Vonda a kiss, then the Ferrises, even as I ignore my father. But it's hard not to catch the anger on Bianca's face, to enjoy it like a long drink of cold water on a hot day.

The curtain falls with a jerking thud, the weights in the bottom hitting the stage so hard I jump. But I'm laughing, it's hilarious, isn't it? I'm not the only one who finds it funny, the cast giggling along with me.

Malik hugs me, Amber hugs me, Aleah is there and she hugs me. And then the curtain is lurching its way up again and the applause is even louder as we step out and bow while the audience shows us how much they love us.

Two more curtain calls and the applause finally goes quiet, the sound of people talking on the other side muffled by the worn velvet curtain. I'm spun around and embraced so many times I know I'll have bruises tomorrow, but I don't care, whispering thanks and I love you's into the ears of the cast, the small crew, until it's just Aleah.

She bounces as she hugs me, lets me go with a huge smile.

"Riley Skyley!" Aleah sings my name. "You… woman, you…" She laughs again. "Holy shit, girl."

I held nothing back. And from the vague memories I have of the last hour, I think it worked out for the best.

"That was so much fun," I say, shivering on the inside. "Let's do it again right now."

The others laugh, cheer, volunteer for a second show even as Dae appears. We all fall silent at the look on her face and I feel a sudden thrill of fear. Did I suck after all? No. Moira denies the possibility even as I shake my head. I was awesome.

Awesome.

Dae looks like someone hit her, as though she's had a terrible shock. I go to her, Aleah at my side, touch her arm.

"Dae?" I say, fearful to ask in case she crumbles on me, but worried about her when she lifts her eyes to mine, hers tight and full of an emotion I can't identify. "Are you okay?"

Aleah rubs her back while Dae shakes her head. Nods. Shakes her head again while the cast whispers, their own concern pressing against my back as I keep my focus and caring on our director. No matter what happened, even if we did suck, we're all in this together.

"He came." Dae sways, one hand on her forehead. "Darren Wright is here." Gasps erupt and it takes me a minute to remember he's the critic Dae talked about that first night. The one who canned Bianca. I shiver, then shrug and grin.

"Screw him," I say, while the cast titters behind me.

Dae shakes her head one more time. "No," she says, "you don't understand. I just talked to him."

I refuse to let disappointment have a place in tonight. "Whatever he said," I tell her, turn to the others, "we were fantastic. And we don't need some critic with a bad attitude to tell us otherwise."

A soft cheer this time. Smiles, nods. I feel so powerful now. Nothing can stop me. Not Bianca, not my father, or my love—yes, I still love him—for Miller. And definitely not some New York theater critic who likes to tear people apart for fun.

Dae grabs my hand, a dazed smile appearing on her lips as she finally pulls herself together. "Riley," she says. "He adored you."

He adored...?

I'm deafened by the screaming, jostled by the bouncing, excited cast and crew, by Aleah who grabs me and twirls me around, laughing. I smile, hug Dae when Aleah lets me go.

"That's great," I say, honestly not caring. Though I'm happy for the rest of the cast.

Because I meant every word I said.

Dae's dazed state breaks as she releases me from a monster embrace. "And he thought the play was brilliant."

"Well, of course it was." Aleah kisses her soundly, hands lingering in Dae's hair. "You wrote it."

I leave them to celebrate when I spot familiar faces at the stage door, run to hug Aunt Vonda. She's crying, pulls away with a sniffle, dabs at her cheeks with a tissue.

"Oh, pet," she says. "I'm breathless. That was beautiful."

Susan and Dwight take a turn, Ian's mother

kissing me softly on the cheek, his father hugging me hard, his handsome face reminding me of who and what I lost. I hold their hands before slipping my arm around Aunt Vonda's waist.

"This is for Ian," I tell his parents. "I only wish I could thank him. He was right. This is exactly what I'm supposed to be doing and I wouldn't. Not without him."

Susan cries while Dwight blinks rapidly, holding back his own tears.

I let them go after a short chat, Aunt Vonda, too. Stand still at the sight of my father waiting, silent and dark, at the door.

At first I'm going to just turn, already see me doing it in my mind, my back to him, rejecting him as he rejected me. But I can't bring myself to let our relationship end this way. Not when he came to the show. Even if it means I only have the chance to rub my success in his face.

But Dad's expression is soft, hurt, lonely. He holds out a small bouquet of flowers, daisies and other spring blossoms, hand shaking as I take them from him. Touch the white flowers Ian loved so much as Dad speaks.

"You look just like your mother," he says, voice cracking. "She was so talented." He draws a breath. "And so are you."

My shock is so powerful I almost don't say anything in return. I can't formulate words into coherent sentences. Until he turns away. My hand reaches out, catches his arm and, for the first time, I see him as he truly is. A damaged man with a broken heart.

I hug him on impulse, something I haven't done since Mom died. Dad goes rigid before melting and hugging me back.

"I know it doesn't make up for all the years," he whispers. "But I'm really proud of you."

He pulls away and, leaves me standing there, staring after him with tears in my eyes.

If only he knew, no matter how tonight turned out, those few words are the only ones that can make me cry.

I retreat to my dressing room, hear the others finally packing up, drifting off in twos and threes until the back of the house is quiet and I'm alone but for the couple of crew still resetting the stage for tomorrow.

Daisies wink at me, their soft petals hanging open, bright yellow centers shining like little suns thirsty for the heat and light of the real one. I lift one free of the bouquet Dad brought and stroke my cheek with the soft whiteness and think of Ian.

He comes to me, stands over me, looking at me through the mirror. He looks healthy, happy, as though he was never sick. I don't know where this crisp image of him comes from. I have no experience to draw on to make him look this way. Seeing him as he could have been makes me shiver, wonder at the sight of his handsome face, the way he looks at me with so much love.

Like he's really there.

He raises one hand. Smiles. Blows me a kiss.

Fades away. And I know it's for the last time. Forever.

Laughing, crying, hugging myself as I whisper thank you into the quiet air, I close my eyes.

And I let him go.

# Chapter Thirty

Dae's loft is full of people, crowded with actors and audience, cast and crew. I squeeze my way through the tight hall, accepting yet another round of congratulations, taking offered business cards, endure several people whispering, "call me," as I make my way from the bathroom back into the living room.

Aleah grabs me, hands me a glass of wine, but I only sip it, unable to eat any of the food laid out for the opening night party. I've changed into a little black dress, let my hair down, feet bare. It seems more natural without Moira's makeup on. Like I'm me again, though I can sense her, ready and waiting for me.

It's a great feeling.

I suspect it's going to take a lot of getting used to sharing my soul with the characters I play. But I'm more than excited to see where doing so takes me.

Dae grabs my hand, points at a tall, dark-haired man in the corner. "That's Darren Wright," she hiccups. She's already swaying, though if she's just drunk on alcohol I'd be surprised. We're all a little exhausted from the show, not to mention high on the results. "Do me a favor. Go make nice."

I roll my eyes, but smile and nod. Turn to make my way through the chattering group. I'm about to approach him when I see who he's with.

Bianca's flirting is pathetic to me as I observe her with a critical eye. All coy and bright, tossing her blonde hair, hand resting near her cleavage. Totally transparent in her need to impress, at least to me. A sudden bolt of understanding slices through my awareness. Aleah said once, not so long ago, Bianca was a bitch because she struggled with her confidence. And I can see it now, how false she is, almost desperate to be appreciated. Noticed and loved.

I shift my focus to Darren. To the subtle signs of his irritation. The way he half-turns from her, sips his drink, eyes drifting away as she speaks. I smother a laugh. I called Aunt Vonda a flower whisperer for her understanding of people through the flowers they buy. I'm suddenly seeing what she does, without the need for blossoms in translation.

The view is so clear I feel giddy from it. Even as I'm aware it's not only an understanding, passive and quiet, but a tool. I do have a brief moment of guilt over my need for vindictiveness when it races through me. But Moira, bless her, gives me the edge I need to shunt my old empathies aside.

I'm not going to hurt Bianca. Just teach her a lesson.

With a grin I can't shake, I slip through the crowd and stop at Darren's side.

He glances my way. And smiles, instantly turning his back on Bianca. I encourage him with a soft touch on his elbow. Nothing overt or flirtatious. Relying on my natural generosity and openness to put him at ease. It's almost ridiculous how at ease I feel.

Why did I ever doubt?

I catch Bianca's frozen glare out of the corner of my eye even as I shake Darren's hand.

"Riley James." He releases my hand, his deep voice soft, fingers lifting to slip his wire-rimmed glasses up his nose. "I have to say, I hesitated to come tonight." His hazel eyes are large behind his lenses as he adjusts his leather satchel over his shoulder, drink sloshing. "But Dae was right. You are fantastic." He pulls out a small notebook, a pen. I take his drink from him, smile graciously when he flashes me one of his own. "I understand you're Marie St. Claire's daughter."

"I am," I say without hesitation. "And you're so kind. Thank you for coming. It means so much to the company to know you were in the audience." I mean every word. I know they are still high on his presence. What him loving the show could mean for us.

"Do you have plans once the run is over?" He's almost hunched over me, pen scratching on the page. Bianca tries to sidle between us, opening her mouth to speak, but I tilt my head to shut her out, just a slight turn to my shoulder blocking her slim window.

"Not yet," I say. "Though I hear Miller Hill is writing a new show." I drop that on purpose. Hoping Bianca caught the message loud and clear.

Darren's eyes widen behind his glasses. "Really." I can see him taking mental notes even as he jots physical ones, and I hope this is enough impetus to get Miller to write again, no matter what happens between us. Which makes me think of him and wonder what I'm going to do about us.

If there even is an "us" anymore.

"Well, no matter the role," he says, tucking his book and pen away before shaking my hand again, "I look forward to seeing you perform."

He leaves quickly, bobbing a nod to me.

Avoiding Bianca.

The moment he's gone, she's in my space, staring her hate.

My grin is back. I close the distance between us before she can even muster a word, look her up and down.

"So," I say, drawing out the vowel for full effect. "I hear you think you can act."

And laugh in her face.

The stunned, furious look she gives me is more than enough reward. I turn my back on her and, still laughing, walk away.

Maybe it was cruel. But she had it coming.

Funny, my revenge taken, I suddenly don't feel like being around all these people anymore. The night seems complete—or close to it. There's one more thing I want to do. I just don't know if I have the courage to do it.

I'm on my way to the door, looking for my shoes. Planning what I'm going to say to him. How I'm going to make things right between us.

Knowing I'll be okay even if I can't, but hoping there's still a place for me in his heart.

So intent on my purpose, I almost run into Miller.

It's hard not to jerk back, to stare at him. Is my imagination working again? Or is he really here? He watches me, hesitant, as though he's ready to run. The moment I pull away, he starts to turn, but I grab him, partly to stop him and partly just to touch him so I know he's real.

The moment my fingers latch onto his shirt sleeve, my insides tighten. *Not make believe.*

I don't hesitate, drag him back down the hall, through the press of people, and into the bathroom.

Slam the door shut behind us, leaning against it, breath coming shallow, too quick.

I turn to stare up into his eyes with a million words waiting to be spoken.

Neither of us says a word, not even when someone pounds on the door, telling us to hurry up.

Miller and I both speak at exactly the same moment.

"I'm sorry—"

"It's all my fault—"

We both lurch to a halt. Laugh together, quiet, low.

"You came to the show." I know the answer. I don't have to see the little smile lifting his sad mouth.

"I wouldn't have missed it," he says. "You were everything I knew you could be. More. You were truly incredible."

I swallow hard past the lump in my throat and the burning sensation racing over my skin. I want him to touch me. I need to throw my arms around him. But I can't yet.

Not until we heal this jagged tear between us.

"Riley," he says, taking the first step before I can. "I'm such a jerk."

"Miller," I say. "I'm such a bitch."

Tears trickle from my eyes, though I'm laughing and he's laughing, too.

I lean in, kiss his cheek, the same one I slapped. "I didn't think you'd forgive me for what I did."

He shakes his head. "I didn't think you would, either." His hesitation makes my breath quiver. "She just wanted to hurt you," he said. "And I let her."

More laughter as I shake off my tears. "You helped me," I said. "You loved me when I didn't know what I needed. And you loved her, no matter what she did." If only I deserved the kind of loyalty he showed Bianca.

The kind, I suppose, I showed Ian.

Miller grabs me, pulls me against him. "I love

you, Riley," he says. "I never thought I would love anyone but her. Until I met you. I finally understood it's not really love when the other person just wants to use you and throw you away."

I nod, stroke his jaw with my fingertips. "I'm sorry I didn't trust you," I say. "I have no idea what's coming, but I promise I'll do everything I can to never hurt you again."

Tears rise in his eyes, fall down his cheeks, one landing on the back of my hand. I kiss him gently, feel his body shake. I hug him, pressing my nose into his neck.

"I love you, too, Miller Hill," I say.

Who would have thought, after how long my imagination sustained me, that reality is so much better than anything I could make up.

"I need to tell you so much," Miller whispers.

I lean back, wink at him, hands sliding into his hair, hip leaning into his leg. "We're actors, silly," I say. "No more telling." Roll my eyes for dramatic effect. "Surely you can do better than that."

Miller's eyes sparkle as he bends and presses his lips to mine.

And does his very best to show me exactly how he feels.

# About the Author

Everything you need to know about me is in this one statement: I've wanted to be a writer since I was a little girl, and now I'm doing it. How cool is that, being able to follow your dream and make it reality? I've tried everything from university to college, graduating the second with a journalism diploma (I sucked at telling real stories), was in an all-girl improv troupe for five glorious years (if you've never tried it, I highly recommend making things up as you go along as often as possible). I've even been in a Celtic girl band (some of our stuff is on YouTube!) and was an independent film maker. My life has been one creative thing after another—all leading me here, to writing books for a living.

Now with multiple series in happy publication, I live on beautiful and magical Prince Edward Island (I know you've heard of Anne of Green Gables) with my very patient husband and six massive cats.

I love-love-love hearing from you! You can reach me (and I promise I'll message back) at patti@pattilarsen.com. And if you're eager for your next dose of Patti Larsen books (usually about one release a month) come join my mailing list! All the best up and coming, giveaways, contests and, of course, my observations on the world (aren't you just dying to know what I think about everything?) all in one place: www.bit.ly/pattilarsenemail.

Last—but not least!—I hope you enjoyed what you read! Your happiness is my happiness. And I'd love to hear just what you thought. **A review** where you found this book would mean the world to me—**reviews feed writers** more than you will ever know. So, loved it (or not so much), **your honest review** would make my day. **Thank you!**

www.ingramcontent.com/pod-product-compliance
Lightning Source LLC
Chambersburg PA
CBHW060923180626
46817CB00004B/1369